body sharers

RUTGERS PRESS
fiction

body sharers

A NOVEL

Elisabeth Rose

Rutgers University Press
New Brunswick, New Jersey

Selections from this work have previously appeared in *Feminist Studies*.

Library of Congress Cataloging-in-Publication Data

Rose, Elisabeth, 1963–
    Body sharers : a novel / Elisabeth Rose.
        p.   cm.   —   (Rutgers Press fiction)
    ISBN 0-8135-1934-9
    I. Title.   II. Series.
PS3568.07624B6   1993
813′ .54—dc20   92–28944
                                                                  CIP

British Cataloging-in-Publication information available

for ~~Kim~~
kit

contents

body sharers

What is your substance, whereof are you made,
That millions of strange shadows on you tend?

Shakespeare, Sonnet 53

/ o / n / e /

the
smell
of
indian
dyes

Caught in that hour of paralysis called sleep, when the mind wakes to recognize it, panics, and struggles to regain control, when the mind says "Move," and believes it has been obeyed, only to find itself trapped in its immovable body, when the mind realizes that it's exposed, now not just to this world, but to the next and all the unknowns in between, I prayed that my mother would fold me up in my mattress. Then I realized the phone was ringing. I tried to move an arm, a toe, then felt myself get out of bed and walk down the hall, only to find I was still locked in my body, in my bed. I tried to scream, and heard myself scream; I felt my spine arch and my lungs grow hot. A child, I prayed for my parents to hear the ringing and my panic, to come touch me and free me, but the ringing went on and on. Then I realized we must all be poisoned, bewitched, alone in our own undefinable horror, when suddenly I was freed, wide awake and unified and feeling my way down the hall—doorjamb, picture frame, bathroom door, shaggy carpet underfoot, the dusty rectangle of the den window, the silhouette of the phone.

I answered and through static heard an old woman's voice call me by name. It asked for my mother. The voice called itself my grandmother Modery.

All my grandparents were dead.

A strange mood swelled me so completely as to leave me outside myself—a twelve-year-old girl standing in her green nightgown, chest-high to her father's drawing table, the swing-arm lamp a black wink above her, the streetlight outside casting a thin, diagonal sallowness into the room. The empty mood kept rolling in, and my eyes welled with its insubstantial pressure.

"There is no heaven," the voice said.

The streetlight steeped through my body, an electric sweat.

"No heaven," it said.

I tried to say "Granma!" but my throat made a sound like wet gravel. I sat down on the floor and pulled the phone clanging down beside me.

"Get your mother!" The words formed out of boiling wires, and I waited.

"Get her." The receiver then brought forth only a steady cascade of rasping. I waited on the floor in the camel-colored light, and when the woolen cords of carpet began to itch my legs, I got up. I hung up the phone, put it back in place, and went to bed, sick for sleep.

~

The next morning I told my mother. She listened as she made anisette coffee. She wore her hair bleached blond, shoulder-length and straight, and her face was heart-shaped, her eyes dark brown and deep-set, her lips roundly sweet. Thin, stooped, flat-bottomed yet large-breasted, she wore plain, manly clothes. All the rooms in the house smelled of her perfume, more like the side effect of some other decoration, like the smell of Indian dyes.

She took over my story. "In the night," she said, "sometimes my

father grabs my foot and shakes it and I wake up. He comforts me."
She sat down and took the lid off the sugar bowl.

"You can *see* him?" I broke apart my chocolate Pop Tarts to help
them cool.

She nodded, and spooned the tiniest pinch of sugar granules into
her cup.

"Grandmom asked for you," I said, encouraged.

"Early death runs in the family," she said.

She nodded at me over her cup, and I saw steam snake into each
nostril. "You, you'll live to be ninety, like your father's family." She
was so sexy, so captivating that my eyes fixed on her happily; my
heart lightened whenever she turned her attention on me, especially
when she played her records for me: Steppenwolf, Patti Smith, Edgar
Winter, the soundtrack from *Jesus Christ Superstar*. We sang together
and she held me close, dancing me slow even though the music was
fast.

"I look like you, Mom." I glanced down at my chest, the only
chest budding in the sixth grade. For a moment, I couldn't eat my
breakfast.

"You *look* like me," she said, and I could smell the anisette on her
breath. She smiled, and I remembered her body in the tub with me
some nights, especially her breasts, luxuriously weighty and firm,
with bumpy brown nipples, and the triangular smudge between her
pole-thin legs under the steamy, soap-murky water. I noticed that
while her body shrank over long months of illness, at the same time it
seemed to grow too heavy for her to maneuver, the muscles wilting
under young skin, but in the tub, she seemed strong, lifting handfuls
of water over my head.

"You're too big for this," she laughed. "You used to be my baby
girl. Now you're my sister." And yet she let me stare.

I finished my Pop Tarts and threw out the crusts while she washed
the coffeepot.

"Good morning, ladies," my father said, transforming the kitchen
with his after-shave, his size, his brisk movement, and his suit
smelling of a dry cleaner's. He swung open the refrigerator door, and
it made its wide, white rectangular kiss. He drank down half a bottle
of apple juice, and my mother shook the glass coffeepot, spinning the
soap suds in the window light.

He squeezed her shoulder. "I'm late. Cammie, see you tonight." He kissed my forehead and went out the door.

I asked if Dad saw Granpa when he stood at the end of her bed, and she said no.

∾

My mother died two years later in her sleep. Before leaving for school that day, I went to look for her to say I'd be late coming home because of band practice, and found her curled up in bed next to a heap of blankets and the empty stretch of mattress where my father had slept. She was still warm under the sheet. I did not cover her face. Leftover smudges of her rust eye shadow made grottoes of the lids. Her two ovals of eye shadow had been her art—a jar on a pasture hill, a curtain sewn across a valley, two aesthetically placed strokes that daubed her face—an unhappy and apprehensive woman. I did not cover her face, nor did I cry. I felt for her pulse, I tore the front of her gown so she could breathe, I smacked her hard across the face when I knew she was dead; no blood rose to meet the sting. I pulled back the covers, and the last of her heat lifted, along with the rancid vapor of urine and another headiness that I found pooling under her hips. At first I thought it some discharge of death, but then knew it was part of my father, part of their private world of pills in round blue packets, part of the vague upset of trips to the doctor that had evaporated my brothers, my sisters. I ripped the seams of the pink cotton nightgown until I could slide it from under her so that she could be naked and I could cry. I stood in the light falling from other rooms down the hall, light filtered and reflected, and falling red from behind the shades and through the curtains, and I held the soiled nightgown, which had barely hidden her body as she moved through the house, leaned over the sink to brush her teeth, squatted at drawers to put laundry away, took a package from a nervous UPS man, her breasts wondrous pink vessels, all comfort, all life. I put the fabric in my nightie drawer and got a soapy washcloth and tried to wash her, wondering if I should remove her cracked nail polish and lifting, in the half-light, her terrible legs.

But I didn't know how to bathe her, especially seeing for the first time that it wasn't her flesh that made her sexy, always dying as it was, unable to replenish itself, finally collapsing her lungs, fraying her heart, but her skeleton—infinitely female. Soon the washcloth grew cold in my hand, making me notice I had missed my bus, making me just get on with it and call the ambulance. The ambulance came for me, I knew, because it came fast. It howled through town, shoppers tilted in shop windows like mannequins, traffic halted in the gutters, and telephone lines hung full of nothing but loud panic as I stood in the half-light with my naked mother and saw from above how alarm swooped onto our roof, felt it grip the timber around, squeeze and condense the air; and the helplessness, and the nakedness, and the absence that had always been would not *move*, no matter how I shouted at it.

∾

Four years will pass in no time, Marge thought. As far as she was concerned, there was nothing more to scheme or propose or apologize for. After her mother died, Cam came with her father to explore the house and kennels, check out the room that would be Cam's, sample one of her dinners—steak Diane—and tally monthly costs with Scofield. Cam would live with them while she went through high school. In a few weeks, she would move in with a turbulence of boxes, clothes hangers, and strange smells, uncomfortable eyes. In no time, routine would iron over the dissonance, and Cam, like a new dog, would make her footfalls and eccentricities part of the moil merely by being there.

Cam sat on the couch close to her father, with her fists between her knees. In the dimming window light, she seemed to follow the men's conversation about the gamble of linebreeding, her eyes darting from face to face, nodding, chuckling the very moment the men did. Her makeup too dark, her woolly hair poorly cut and hanging in her eyes, she had the unwieldy prettiness of thousands of other teenage girls. Marge tried to feel motherly, or resentful that this newly motherless child should be palmed off on her by her husband's stepcousin, but felt nothing more than she would have had someone thrown an ice cube into a pot of soup she was heating—it might interfere with the simmer, but eventually the ice would melt and blend with the broth. She pitied the girl her grief for her mother, but suspected that her mother's death was ultimately fortuitous. She figured she should resent Scofield's relative, by distant marriage only, abandoning his little girl, but she couldn't. He said openly that he loved his daughter but had never been a good father, and he wasn't sure he wanted to work at being a better one. "I do think of myself as a husband," he said, "and I don't want her to see me wife-shopping." Marge envied him his bold claim to freedom and his unencumbered travels, and she admired his daughter because she admired almost anyone with hardships, never curious about how they coped, never disdainful of those who broke down, as long as they kept moving forward in their own time, not slowing her down. Young, Cam apparently carried on well in her strife, responding to dependency and her father's double cross with a straight-backed, flat-eyed indifference.

Marge excused herself and went to the kitchen, agitated by the dirty dishes and the sick Doberman puppies. With about forty police dogs to raise, train, and sell and so many whelping, she, Scofield, and their regular hand Sweeney couldn't know each one intimately enough to anticipate illness. Kennel cough wracked half of them half the time. She thought perhaps the Doberman bitch's milk had soured, which meant she'd have to bring the puppies into the house and bottle-feed them, or divide the litter among surrogates. The effort almost wasn't worth it. Perhaps they'd heal themselves. Besides, she knew she was likely to have forgotten about them by the time she was done with the dishes.

All her life she had had an incessant desire simply to get to the next point. As a child walking to school, she consumed herself with a drive to pass the next telephone pole, turn the next corner, step over the next weed. Birthdays gave her immense relief. Marriage, a major object, left her disoriented, goalless for months. She crossed days off her calendar with accomplishment, a treasure hunter of time increments. When she was older, she saw her hurried living more as a habit than a worthwhile drive. It made only suicidal sense to hurtle her impatient self through life, and she wasn't suicidal. She did not intend to charge through the final goalposts of death, throw down the pigskin, and jog there in circles to the sound of horns, but to scramble, maybe halfheartedly, the other way. Whatever the reasons for living her life in a fuss, the momentum was fixed, and it was good. Cam's four years with them would be short.

$\sim$

Scofield's K-9 City, where I went to spend my high school years, spanned seven acres of farmland, uncultivated, dipping steep with tiny hillsides, full of gnarled, ancient vine-draped trees. Scofield employed several hands, from two teenage feed-and-clean-up boys to a seventy-year-old trainer. In dozens of whitewashed kennels and runs, he bred and raised police dogs, mostly German shepherds, and placed the pups with local volunteer families for one year. Then he began their basic training. People who wanted family guard dogs, 4-H youths, and cops who wanted to know their dogs from puppyhood met with their puppies for obedience classes. The pups were taken out to the practice field—leveled into an open hillside and mowed like a golf green—and taught *heel, sit, down-stay,* and *come.* During odd hours, one of Scofield's men poison-proofed the young dogs with morsels of dead mice and dead rabbit and cubes of steak plopped into inviting spots and subtly wired with an electric charge. More accomplished dogs ran manhunts, learned to attack, fetched dropped firearms, sniffed out drugs, searched abandoned homes and warehouses, and leapt for cover under fire. When finished with all the training, the dogs were loyal to their masters despite even extreme abuse. Scofield was proud of his blue-ribbon bloodlines, proud of his training and retraining programs, and defiant about the frequent charge from townspeople that many of his dogs turned out to be indiscriminate biters and ended up in pounds, glue factories, and laboratories, or in chicken coops and sheep corrals, shot dead.

People said that so many of his biting dogs had been turned loose by frightened, exasperated owners that the forest was now lorded over by a pack of savage dogs—blood-matted German shepherds, scarred and lip-curling Dobermans, steer-killing mastiffs—who trotted snarling through the nights, who had mauled and eaten a nine-year-old boy, who were so wise and well trained, so varied in size and skill that they could raid homes, track down, kill, and bury whole hunting parties, and halt moving cars and slaughter the occupants. Rural children never played outside after sunset, and adults who went out at night took their guns. My favorite rumor was this: Some said Wild Julia led the pack—a girl who had been gang-raped by local boys, then beaten by her father and raped again when she told him what the boys had done. She finally disappeared, insane, gone to live with the pack. Naked, she rode a Great Dane and kept her hair twisted and clumped in a rope down her back. She killed and ate with the dogs, and by day slept under their spittle-strung jowls. The dogs were ordered to kill and eviscerate on sight any woman—the source of all putrefaction.

When I went to live with Scofield and his wife Marge, I still hated him. When I was four I had hated him so much my grandmom started taking me to church to teach me not to be unruly, to teach me to pray for others. All I remembered of him was that, when I stayed at his house once when I was four, he had gotten angry at me in the bathroom, so angry that he shook me and wouldn't give me dinner. I was afraid of Scofield, my father said to me when I was still little, only because he was big and dark, and we didn't talk to him or his wife for years because they didn't like my mother, who could be a bitch.

~

Scofield stands over a Doberman bitch and her suckling litter of six pups. He can get more than a thousand dollars for each, and he hopes the light-colored runt, climbing stupidly over its brothers who clamber on their mother's ribs, will have sense enough not to let the others starve it. He picks it up and pushes its face at the drier teats in the soft flesh under the bitch's lifted thigh. "They do just as good," he says, but now the pup is too frightened to feed. When he sees it cower, he cracks it in the face with two fingers and says, "Second thought, hope you starve." Camille comes crunching through the dead leaves, which crackle along the ground all year, and makes her way toward him down the clamorous row of kennels, ignoring the dogs' deadly lunges, the snarls, and mouths snapping like living leg-hold traps. Whenever a particularly vicious shepherd, mastiff, or bloodhound throws itself against its gate, she says "Hi."

"Don't you make 'em go soft on me now," he shouts. He watches her grin, and thinks vaguely that nothing could go soft near her. He has seen her roll in the grass with his dogs, laugh as they lick her nose and teeth, wrestle them with her bare arms, the blunt-faced, bone-breaking Rottweilers, the wicked, raw-muscled Dobermans, silly with their wet, pinkfinger hard-ons. When she reaches him he hugs her over his belly. She is nearly as tall as he.

He decides to have her help him work one of the dogs. When he works them in front of her, he feels impressive, not so intimidatingly overweight. His belly is the barrel of his status, and no man his age of any consequence goes without one. But around her, so young and busty, he would rather be athletic than imposing.

He likes having her in the small ring with the nine-foot chain-link fence and the neat coil of barbed wire around the top. He dreams of pulling her screaming, sometimes laughing, from the mesh, her hands bloodied from the barbs—there is some nondescript but energetic struggle with clothing, then she is on her face in the dirt and he hauls her round white hips up under his belly and she is tight and unyielding, but after a stab or two he comes long and grinds his breath through his teeth, there, kneeling in the center of his dirt ring. She, limp, rolls away from him and smiles; her clothes have vanished, her pubescent legs are spread wide, her hands outstretched and bleeding; she wants him again.

He fixes old, friendly Gottfried up in a choke chain and hands the leash to Cam. Now she knows how to handle a dog. Lately she talks more openly with him and Marge at dinner, and she says maybe she'll go to veterinary school, maybe she'll be an animal behaviorist, maybe she'll train Seeing Eye dogs. "Why not police dogs?" Marge asked her the night before. "Too much competition," Cam said, and smiled kind of at Scofield's chest. One of her first jokes with them, and Marge had not laughed but nodded to herself, thinking, he knew, now we're getting somewhere with this sullen, freaky little cat.

∾

Sometimes I would read *The Girl in a Swing* until late at night, or stare at the model on the cover and trace her makeup to see how she got her pale face to rise out of gauzy blackness like that, and when Uncle Scofield and Aunt Marge had long stopped their jumbles of talk and the dogs were quiet outside and the refrigerator and the heat left the house still but for the few chilled crickets mechanically piping and the powdery rattle of a moth at my pane, I pulled the torn panels of pink cotton from my bottom drawer and waited on the floor by the hall phone. Once I fell asleep there under the hall table, and Uncle Scofield found me at the blackest hour, the moon down and no light. Even though I said I was all right, he meant to carry me back to bed but couldn't lift me, the old hallway so narrow and uneven, and the little telephone table so invisible. I stood, and he swung me up into his arms. Strange, I thought, to be floatingly portable.

He found my bed and laid me in its lumpiness, uneven like the old floorboards, the narrow, twisted stairs, the popping kitchen linoleum, the knotted, tumbling lawns. Then he sat on the edge beside me, and I braced myself to keep from falling against him, and he breathed there, my father's cousin yet strange to me, dark-haired as he was, and dark-skinned, his fingernails thick as beetles. In what small light fell from the astral dust and stars, his cheek floated in my vision, a soft woodborer pale, flecked with the dirt of black whiskers. A wide hand made its firm way down my spine and then repeated its path, a stroke for sick dogs. I said I was all right, and yet it continued. I said stop it, and the hand made one more slow trip and stopped at my bottom.

"You're gonna be okay, kid." His voice took a growl to get started, the black quiet was so thick. He patted me on the bottom. "You can talk to Marge and me if you need something." The rumble of his voice ground my ears with irritation. He left, and his heat and sleep-sweat pressed over my bed, violating my nostrils.

Whenever I kept my dark night vigils on the floor by the hall phone, I walked, in my mind, through my mother's house. Although I lived there all my life and my father lived with us, the house was mostly hers because she perfumed it. I sat under the hall table in the dark, wrapped in my terry cloth robe, with her nightgown in a plastic bag on my lap, waiting. I held the bag to my nose with my fingers wrapped around its neck, letting only the tiniest filament of odor escape. In the silken weave I discovered the smells of her underarms, the delicate waft of her breasts and stomach, the brown tanginess of her forearms, the silk fabric itself, the unlaundered sheets, my father, her soap, her deodorant, her vagina, sperm, urine, sweat, the very sweet fragrance of dead mammal, and her perfume—patchouli— overpowering it all. Concentrating alone in the dark, I could identify all these odors, and through them my imagination gave me the memory of her body. Her dead body was a good place to start, but I had to fight through it, beyond it, to get to her house, where I could perhaps reach her soul. I focused on the patchouli, the essence and breath of the house, but that fragrance deadened olfactory cells. Lots of strong odors do that. If you put your nose to a lilac and sniff, the odor will fade, giving the impression that you've inhaled all the scent from the flower, when really you've only deadened your own cells. Patchouli faded fast, so I had to climb out of her body quickly and get into the house. If I lost it too soon, I panicked, afraid of smothering in the loss, my mind transported in the wrong direction through a heavy rain of paramedics, one—a woman—hugging me and me letting her, thinking stupid stupid woman, my blood pressure, my heart looking for shock, my father's eyes incredulous, his hands clenching each other, poor stupid Daddy, the phone ringing and ringing because people with only sorry stupid things to say are calling and calling and my friends aren't calling because they're young enough to suspect they're stupid and I call Mr. Dheil every day and say please let me come over.

But some nights I managed to get past her body without losing her perfume, and I stepped out of her bedroom into the quiet, quiet house where light shifted muted red through puffing curtains and big silent leaves. Without footfall I walked, because when not living, you can see and smell, but not hear. Sight and smell are mystical, mysterious, but hearing with its eardrums and clumsy sound waves is a mechanical harassment only of the living. Even in silent living moments, the ringing of your own body is deafening, and in old age you grow deaf in the higher frequencies because of years of exposure to your own body sound.

In the house, in my mind, in the odor of patchouli, I walked room to room in the higher realm of silence and memorized every object and texture. I saw the dusty baseboards, and they did not knock and gurgle. I saw the linoleum in the front hallway, and I knelt down to inspect its swirling blue pattern. I rolled on the living room carpet and laughed at the happy maroon stripes of the velvet couch. I floated to the ceiling and pressed my back, arms, and legs to it. From there I saw the mahogany coffee table, a lovely rectangle of reddish brown oil. I saw the brass angels on the mantel, the dusky Indian rug on the wall, the antique sitar with its stained leather and intricate beadwork, the heavy swing and fall of the valances and drapes. My mother was not downstairs. I bumped along the ceiling and bubbled up the hollow stairwell until I hit the upstairs ceiling. Maybe I would find her in the guest room watching TV with a book in her lap leaning *Mom* back in the old green chair from the days before I was born your ivory robe buttoned up to the top and tucked between your thighs your hair *Mommy* behind your ears unself-conscious falling thinly over your shoulders your chin doubling a little with the angle of your head *Mommy* your feet are in their scuffs propped on the old leather hassock what are you watching *Mommy* what are you reading oh my God oh my God I'll stay right here on the ceiling if you promise not to move and never to look at me.

"Be a good little niece and take your bath," he said. The heavy water hammered into the deep porcelain tub. He knelt on the warped linoleum, and she stood still shorter than he, a tiny four-year-old girl in a red calico dress, leaning against the bright gold and orange flowers of the wallpaper

"I can wash myself, you know," Cam said with conviction, although her shiny red lips pressed together as if about to cry.

"Uncle Scofield can wash you better," he said, and turned off the water and the sound, so that the air was suddenly widely quiet except for the *toink* of a stray drop from the mouth of the hot spigot into the deep pool, the old wooden floorboards creaking under the weight. It was filled high enough to lap up to his breast were he to get in, high enough to heat his thighs and stomach and to make his neck sweat. He churned the water with his arm to mix it and to feel the body of water give way to his muscle. Outside the bathroom, Master, his ancient collie, audibly snuffled, then lay down against the closed door with a grunt, his long red fur poking underneath .

She stood there just like that, with her back to the shiny gold flowers and the fabric of her dress pulled up and scrunched in her fists. "I can wash myself," she said. "Aunt Marge can wash me." But she started to take off her dress, because Aunt Marge wasn't home. He helped her with the buttons in the middle of the small, flat span of her upper back. She held up her hair for him ladylike, and he told her how dear she was and he felt great and gentle and he kissed her smooth baby neck and let his hot breath comfort her, and the heat from the tub rose up through the floorboards, through his folded legs, and burned the cock folded in his shorts.

"Uncle Scofield needs a bath too," he said, and he lifted her body, a white bundle of calfskin, and lowered it into the water and rising steam. She kicked and whimpered like rapid chuckles but then stood silent, hip-deep in the steam. He stripped quickly, and the water rose around her waist as he climbed in beside her. He lathered her body so fast he nearly knocked her down, slipping his big fingers under her arms, into her bare little peach, into her creased bottom, her skin under the white suds red from the heat, his skin thumping and sweating beads. He poured baby oil over his right hand and then again churned the water with his arm. He tried to keep his eyes open on her as he worked; she stood between his outstretched legs, her mouth open, her eyes fixed on what he was doing; the soapsuds licked their way down her chest, the water lapped and sucked at her hips. Then he moaned, and the water quieted and was much cooler. Outside the bathroom, Master rolled over, dragging away the fringe of fur that lined the bottom of the door. Scofield leaned his back and arms along the cold white lips of the tub.

≈

I needed something—to get off the farm. "Take a walk in the woods," Aunt Marge said. "Take a dog along." Dogs cured everything. I said I wanted to help her fix dinner. "It's easier for me to do it. Why don't you cuddle some puppies?" Aunt Marge was short, round, and busy. She went away nearly every weekend to dog shows and conferences and business meetings. She wore aprons, carried briefcases, and snapped the chains of bull terriers. "Play your flute. I'd love to hear it," she said, rubbing a steak with marinade.

She and Scofield agreed when they got married never to have children. Now they had me.

"Do you know the facts of life?" she said one afternoon, sitting next to me on the couch while I practiced my flute. *The Girl in a Swing* lay on the cushion beside me, and she picked it up.

"My mother told me," I said. "That book has some sex in it too."

She widened her eyebrows and put the book down. "No telling what your mother said." She scowled carefully, and I looked at how her eyebrows and lips were penciled onto her skin. "Any questions?"

"It's hard for me to ask." A moodiness squeezed my windpipe and moistened my nose. She said something encouraging, but I could tell we were supposed to bustle through this, too. If I didn't say something now, we might never talk about it again. "What about God?" I said, and covered my reddening nose and trembling chin with my hand.

She hissed air through her lips and teeth. "If you want one there is one." She patted my leg and then shook the paperback at me. "Get rid of the smut," she said.

"It's a ghost story."

"Like hell it is."

≈

Perhaps he and Marge should adopt a little girl, he thought. He would adore a little girl he could think of as his own: the impulsive warmth, the ignorant neediness, the uninformed trust, the purity of mind and skin. She stood in the water between his legs with her arms bent high against her chest, like a baby or someone long paralyzed. Her lips had blued, her skin goose-pimpled, and the soap suds had made their way down her body and married themselves to the water. Something about her blind stare made him look closely at her and forget himself. He felt on the verge of a new level of experience, a love at once pure, sexual, incestuous, fatherly.

She narrowed her eyelids. "God hates you," she said. Her eyes fixed on the mucousy blobs and strings rocking in the water between them, and she gagged over them, heaving and trembling and sweating, straining her tiny shoulders around the noise. He leapt out of the tub, out of the way, but only saliva and some coin-sized circles of bile slid off her tongue. He remembered he was supposed to feed her dinner before her bath, and he felt guilty and stupid and now he could nurture the sick darling, but then he remembered what she had said.

"All right, enough!" he shouted, and grabbed her by the shoulders and hauled her out. Her expression told him she knew everything somehow, that she was capable of saying anything, telling anyone, at the most malicious time. She was a changeling, wise and evil, and her coyness had been seduction, her choking had been staged. She had cursed him and betrayed him. He knelt before her and shook her by the arms. "What does God have to do with an uncle loving his niece like a daughter, God made you filthy because you don't appreciate your uncle washing you clean like you never were, you wicked little shit, I washed filthy places that no one ever washed before, God hates YOU and makes you choke, you naked little faker!"

As punishment, he stood over her and made her scrub the bathtub, then put her to bed without feeding her. He had left her alone in the guest room for some time before he heard her scream down the hallway that if he ever did that again she would tell.

～

When I was nine, I took flute lessons from Mr. Dheil. He was in his sixties, a retired concert guitarist and pianist, a friend of a friend of the family, and an amateur photographer. Once a week I walked to his house three blocks away, with seven dollars in my pocket. I walked home with fifteen.

We spent twenty minutes going over my lessons, and then another hour or so working on my portfolio. He loved me, and wanted great things for me because I was beautiful, he said. If I hadn't practiced enough during the week, he could get very angry, and threatened to stop loving me. At first, before he grew to love me, he just brushed out my hair, giving each stroke great attention. Then, after we had become best friends, he offered me a job modeling for him, as long as I told no one. I wasn't old enough for a work permit. He showed me pictures he had taken of nude women, professional models, and I posed like them. He took his clothes off too, to make me more comfortable, he said. One day he loved me so much that he got on the bed with me and held me and then very firmly held me down and pushed himself inside me. He did this every time after that, because we were lovers now, he said.

By the time I was thirteen, I had several hundred dollars saved, and got pregnant. Mr. Dheil got mad at me—I had promised to tell him when I got my first period, but it never happened. Instead, I had morning sickness and a thickening waist, and Doctor Harris said I was nearly six months gone. Mr. Dheil decided I had to have an abortion, or he and I, our love and my career, his business and my family, would be ruined. I figured an abortion was something that happened to you, as it had happened to my mother, so I spent my money that way. He took me to New York to see the Philharmonic and posed as my irate grandfather. When the baby came out, it was big. No one said anything to me, but I think it lived. When my mother died and I told him I was moving away, Mr. Dheil cried with me and took me out, and we pooled our money and bought me my own solid silver flute.

≈

If Marge could get Scofield to do the laundry this afternoon, perhaps she would have an hour to lead Deputy around and break him of the sudden unexplained spooking, wincing, cringing, before the time came to go. And it was about time Cam earned her keep; there was no reason she couldn't dust instead of collecting it, sitting on that couch with sheet music like layers of white shale all around her. If only people would help, Marge wouldn't waste so much time staring at her timetable dreaming.

Just yesterday she took her three weimaraners to practice in the show ring, and they behaved ribbon-winningly except for Deputy, who acted guilty or beaten or both without bites or bruises anywhere on his hide. She needed some more time with that dog before the camper got packed up to go by five o'clock. She was taking only the weims to this show. Three dogs were enough in the camper; they loved it; she loved it; the lot of them sharing a narrow den, working together, and the tall, muscular horizontal crowd of Bouviers, boxers, and briards, pyrenees, pointers, and mastiffs, wood and water, wool blankets and cages, and hundreds and hundreds of working-class paws around them. All the wet noses trembled.

If she worked Deputy next to the house, she could dash back and forth to the laundry room. Deputy could practice his *stay*. She needed a cleaning woman. As far as Marge was concerned, Cam needed some new sheet music, but Marge knew she wouldn't play it—she played the same ten or fifteen pieces again and again, her fingers and throat flying into the same gullies and over the same ripples and lifts, the same steam lining the inside of her flute. Now she was playing that halting overture, written to be clumsy and arresting, to seize and drive, a tune that stayed with Marge all day but would not allow itself to be hummed or whistled, so that it echoed in the skull with no outlet. Marge remembered she had to leave Cam and Scofield dinner and couldn't recall what she meant to make, and she opened the fridge and there it already sat, foiled over in a casserole dish. She had made it late last night. Her deepest fear was to discover that something significant had been blocked out of her memory: a much older brother lost in the navy, a child given up for adoption.

She pulled her sun cap off the nail by the kitchen door and walked across the grass to fetch Deputy and a show lead. For the past thirty years straight, she thought, her feet had been rooted to the ground, rooted to wood, linoleum, cement, cotton sheets, one day resting in a velvet box. How wonderful it would be to cross these knotted yards to the kennel by gathering a horse's power under and behind her with her legs, to feel it bunch beneath her and contain itself lightly in her hands, the saddle imperceptible. Each rolling hip and shoulder under her pulled her by her squeezing calves, back hanging straight, body poised and balanced, one with the animal, which strode in long-limbed strength, its spine arched with the delicacy of a cat. With neck-catching, hair-whipping speed they'd thunder over the ground, the motion music flowing, lilting, flying her, lifting her by every blood-driving tube in her flesh.

Now, she had dogs instead of one horse, and she was rooted to the ground. She had four rows of kennels and thoughts of a fifth, and couldn't remember where she'd stored her saddle. The power, divided by forty, padded over and dug into and whelped on her earth. The power no longer drove against braided leather reins, strong yet contained lightly, like wind against sailcloth; it held itself encircled by a simple slip chain, or by a show lead, no more bracing than a shoelace.

~

"Brad, Kyle, Sean," Mr. Dheil said as he let the three men in the door.

"I remember," I said. "Hi."

"Hey, Lolita!" Brad said, and he gave me a bear hug, carrying me into the living room.

"Why can't we do this at night?" Kyle said. He wore a tweed jacket, even though the last of the snow had melted and the temperature hit well over fifty. When he spoke, a small iciness burst in my stomach and fanned slowly under my lungs. He had thin black hair and a handsome face dusted with white stubble, and he wore a wedding band and expensive, creaseless shoes.

Even though I was really too big for it, Brad spun around with me in the open living room, past the piano, the hide-a-bar, and the glossy framed print of sheet music reflected in a trumpet. He visited Mr. Dheil and me once a month or so, and called me his little girl, sat me on his lap. He did look a bit like an overweight version of my father, with the gray sideburns blending into a shaggy brown beard.

Sean was Mr. Terrence, the typing instructor from my junior high. He showed up only rarely, said hardly a word, but spoke to me warmly in the hallways at school and talked to the other teachers, counselors, and band directors of my social and academic promise. He was an amateur photographer like Mr. Dheil, which was how he met Brad, who worked in advertising, and Kyle, who shot the occasional model but usually did stills for computer chip companies.

Brad put me down, reached for the snacks on the coffee table, and tilted a fistful of peanuts into his mouth. He and Mr. Terrence sat down on the couch, but Kyle strolled to the piano to read the name on it.

"Nights are so much better for me," Kyle said.

Mr. Terrence took a handful of peanuts, and Brad had one palm heaped with them. There were a few left, but Mr. Dheil had made me brush my teeth right before they arrived.

"C'mere, Leda," Brad said, and slapped his knee with his free hand.

With a bottle tilted above three glasses, Mr. Dheil asked the men if red wine was okay, and I asked him in a near whisper if I could have some peanuts and brush my teeth again. "No," he said, "drink this." He gave me a half-shot of whiskey. "Now."

"Lola," Brad said. I watched Mr. Dheil pour the wine. He glanced down at me several times, then winked. The frost in my belly had traced its way all through my body cavity. I swallowed the whiskey. "Twiggie," Brad said.

Mr. Dheil handed me one glass of wine and said to take it to Brad. He balanced the other two between the fingers of one hand, raising them over my head as he walked by. Brad thanked me by cuddling me into his bosom, ruffling my hair and sweatshirt with his salty hands. "I love you dressed like this," he said.

Mr. Terrence sat on the edge of the couch, eating one peanut at a time out of his hand. I felt sorry for him, since I knew he couldn't help coming here and he honestly liked me. When adults at school said they heard good things about me, I knew they had been listening to him. I rested on Brad's body as he leaned back on the couch, and caught the whoosh of his breath in his windpipe, the slow thump of his heart, and the syllables of his speech muted through his flesh. Mr. Dheil stood near the piano, its finish protected from the afternoon sunlight by a drape, and spoke to Kyle about the effects of steam on his camera. Kyle no longer seemed irritated by the time of day, and he rapidly choreographed a shower scene while Mr. Terrence and Brad spoke more loudly about a bus drivers' strike. Buried in the heavy arms, I felt no cancerous frost crawling when Kyle glanced at me, shaping in the air one sitting on the toilet, one on the shower step, one kneeling in the stall amid steam and the beating hot water, my entrance, our convergence in the spray, a three-in-one. Brad kissed my forehead. I wanted Mr. Terrence to see the affection in that kiss. The more Mr. Dheil spoke of steam and lenses, the drier I felt.

"Black and white," Mr. Dheil suggested.

"God, yes," Kyle said.

Mr. Dheil turned away from Kyle, and I thought good, he hates him, he's tired of him. "Upstairs," Mr. Dheil said to us, and we stood up. I had to pee, and I announced this like a child, to humor Brad. When I came out of the downstairs powder room, Mr. Terrence waited by the door.

"I have to pee too," he said. "Everybody's upstairs."

~

The dogs ducked their heads and whistled in their throats when they saw Marge. "Hi kids," she said. "Hi Joya, how are the wee ones?" Deputy did not come to the chain-link like the others, but sat with his nose lifted, watching her sideways like a bird or a horse. Joya's water dish was empty. "Tim!" she hollered. "Tim!" Now she'd never leave on time. She should have put the laundry in before coming out to get Deputy. On the distant hillside she could see Scofield and Coach Bill gesturing to about ten cops standing in a row with their dogs, shoulder to thigh. Tim was with them.

"What is it, Mrs. Scofield?" Harry, a short-legged, long-torsoed, dimwitted teenager, had jogged up behind her.

"*Why* is this dish empty?" She could hear Cam's flute overture, either through the house and the glass and over the lawns, or else it was trapped in her mind again, bumping against the sides like a fly.

"The camper's about ready, Ma'am." He shrugged at the dish.

"Fill it. Check all the water."

"Tim's helpin' Mr. Scofield."

"I want to leave at five," she said, and wondered strongly if she hadn't been saying that all day, to herself and everyone else, to the dogs and the dirty underwear—How are you, Mrs. Scofield—I want to leave at five—Did you receive our catalogue—I want to leave at five—until it emptied of its topicality and became a minuet.

She gave Deputy and each of the other weims in the run a Liv-A-Snap. Deputy slipped his neck through the show lead and waited for Marge to fasten it tight, but Marge paused to watch Harry leaning over the spigot while the water drummed into the metal can. The dogs lifted their lips around the cracker fragments, and three sets of teeth clapped in unison. Harry had been with them about eight months, but seemed suddenly very at home, as though he now ate there. He had thick shoulders, and his long back came to a narrow waist. He was inoffensive and believed with his whole small mind in hopping-to. She recalled that he was on the high school swim team, had a number of odd jobs, and came from a poor but good family. He screeched the spigot off, swung the heavy can from the ground, and disappeared around the end kennel. She no longer wanted to leave at five; she didn't want to leave the sound of the redundant flute; as long as she could hear the music, she knew Cam was alone and behaving herself. But Marge had paid her entry fee and the camper was ready and the dogs—all but Deputy—were ready, and she was going even though a faint alarm sat in her stomach and a prickle of sweat under her arms, and she knew and the dogs knew that nothing was to be trusted about Cam.

~

I knew at fourteen that there were many channels between the living and the dead or nonliving. The main channel was the vagina, into which the nonliving reached like a knitting hook in the form of a finger, ear of corn, penis, vibrator, hairbrush, and eventually sperm— the only hook that could break through to the dead and pull forth a thread of life, which ultimately resulted in a corpse, either before birth or sometime after. The main purpose of my body was indulgence, not in the form of feeding or intoxicating but in moving it and having it looked at. I could fascinate myself with my appearance—the only way I could have an orgasm was to dance or stretch in front of the mirror, never even touching my clitoris, or to stand with a blanket draped over me and expose various parts of my body to the glass.

Death and sex were topics never to be discussed with any other woman, which is why when Marge asked if I knew about the facts of life I couldn't say, yes, I had a baby, what about you? But any subject, especially sex, was fair game in certain situations for most males older than me. Boys my age or younger, and girls too, were to be kept innocent of these ideas at all costs and with fury. I couldn't explain this decorum, but I understood it was natural. I kept no secrets, but lived without revealing my mind to women, understanding that to do so would be to suffer their disdain. Certain men too, you could just tell immediately who they were, fell into the category with women—people who would torture me with contempt if they knew my life. Aunt Marge was of course in this category, but Uncle Scofield fell into none of them—he was half scorn-wielder and half body-sharer. Most of the men at the farm, especially the policemen, were body-sharers too.

I could watch myself in my mind in order to come. I could remember myself in the movies with Mr. Dheil and his friends, although I never once came when he or any of them touched me. Movies and memories are perfect for coming, because they are nonliving, and the only tools to access a female orgasm are nonliving, because an orgasm is chemical. I could walk and concentrate on my walkingness and come. I could sit on the couch with Aunt Marge and Uncle Scofield, between the darkness of the room and the flash of the TV, and concentrate on the nonlife of the couch and my clothes, the squeeze of my crotch in my jeans, the motion of breathing and tensing; I could come sitting up against these two people, which was perfect because of the contrast between my machinery and the life of their unknowing scorn. If they noticed me shiver and Aunt Marge asked if I was cold, I said that I was.

～

For a while, Father Robert noticed a woman with white hair like a molded blast of frost coming to Mass daily with a brown-haired little girl. The child's hair, he thought, was all springs and vines of unruliness, and someone, the white-haired woman or the child's mother, was forever trying to snap it down with pink plastic clips or with bits of elastic with baubles attached. Out of the eight or ten people at daily Mass, Father Robert noticed the richly wild-haired girl because she never looked at him or at the crucifix. Once, during the Eucharist, he caught her glancing his way, and he gestured to Christ hanging crucified above him, and she looked down at her hands, and didn't move her eyes again.

That day after the service, he greeted parishioners as they left. The woman introduced herself. "Anne Modery," she said. Under the white hair, her face was smooth. "M'granddaughter Camille . . ." she slid her hand into the hair of the girl buried in the hem of her coat ". . . who's shy."

Something made him want to inspect the little body for bruises, sift through the bales of hair for bumps, lift the eyelids like gauze from

her painful eyes and search them. Perhaps the frost-haired woman
was guilty, like the woman with quivering eyeballs he tried to reason
with at the St. Francis Center for Abused Children just a month
before. She had repeatedly locked her little daughter in a toy chest
and sent it crashing down the cellar staircase. He went to speak to
Monsignor about Camille.

"I can just tell. I've watched her cower."

"You have no reason. No witness has come forward." Monsignor
looked tired of Father Robert already. He sat hunched over in his
robes, his lean small body bent as though once obese. He had the face
of a fat man, bulging cheeks and drooping jowls. His eyes were two
dark blue, wet smears. Father Robert often felt he made the old man
tired just by standing near him, his body by contrast well fed and well
proportioned, built for endurance and motion. "I'll tell you what you
do have," Monsignor said. "Undirected energies."

He told Father Robert to spend less time hanging around the
Center filling his head with the horrors of child abuse. "You can
know too much, you know," he said. And Father Robert knew too
little about Anne Modery and her granddaughter, too little to do a
thing.

For two years Anne Modery came to Mass daily with Camille, and
when the child reached school age, Father Robert saw her only on
Sundays. By the time Camille was nine or ten, she bore the look of
someone staring in a mirror; her walk and poise and expression had
an absorbed self-awareness. A rapt viewer, she compelled everyone to
watch as she knelt slowly, the knee curving under her wool skirt, her
head bowed as her eyes targeted the kneeler, her bobbed hair clamped
back in a headband.

When Father Robert heard that Anne Modery, dead of a heart
attack at age fifty-eight, was to be memorialized at the Methodist
church, he told the minister, and then Anne's family, that she'd been
coming to daily Mass for the last half-dozen years. Everyone shrugged.
She had married a Methodist, and she and her husband had plots in
the Methodist cemetery; Mr. Modery wanted it that way. At Camille's
house, he asked her parents, what about Camille? She should be put
in the Catholic school, he said. She's fine where she is, the father said
from his gray three-piece suit. She doesn't have many friends, the
mother said from the couch, her bare feet on the coffee table. There,
Father Robert saw the shape of Camille's little legs; in the woman's
face he saw Camille's face. It would be cruel to take her from her few

friends and from the school band, the mother said. Her printed cotton skirt was rumpled high on her lap, and her perfume oppressed the air. She had the slow smile of flower power, which made Father Robert look incredulously at the man in the three-piece suit. He and the couple fell quiet, and the room filled with such absurdity that he thought surely they all would laugh.

~

Sitting on the floor in front of Scofield's TV, I heard on the news that the earth lost plots of trees at the rate of a football field a second. This contributed to the greenhouse effect. Mother Earth was going bald, dying. Cancer of the scalp. Many healthy men went bald because they were supposed to. I figured testosterone was responsible, habitually overindulging the lower body with its hair gifts, and skimping on top. As a little girl, I had cupped in my hands men's mossy skulls and looked down on them while their jaws chewed my hairless crotch. I couldn't understand why some women sincerely found testosterone-sheared heads attractive. Hey, Aunt Marge, I wanted to say, why do you suppose some women like bald men when it's the same thing that happens to buzzards? But Aunt Marge would just say she didn't know, and I couldn't shake off the thought of a red ear cupped against each inner thigh, and the woman on the news went on about industry, toxic waste, and a hole in the ozone.

Testosterone now fleeced sections of my torso and legs, and I raked my razor over my armpits and calves, leaving just the hair on the pubis. I mowed it down, not at the rate of a football field a second, but it all amounted to the same kind of ruin, I thought. We had streamlined the world so that it was simple, efficient, and malignant. A hole punched in the atmosphere seemed to equal a hole punched in the bottom of one's only boat, and that, to mankind, was better, simpler, than the kaleidoscope of ecosystems razed. We are dying, I thought, and I was happy in the splash of blue television light.

~

One of the kids who worked for Scofield after school and week-ends could have been my older brother. He looked like me as he hefted sacks of Purina and shot crap off the cement with the jet from the hose. Leaning against the shed, he smoked a cigarette, and, since locusts thickened the hazy air with their song and the oak leaves glinted like chrome, I decided to introduce myself. When he saw me, he showed me the cigarette. "Lunch," he said, with a look of apologetic self-pity.

I offered to make him a sandwich, but Tim said he had to lose weight. To me, he seemed as slender as a girl, but instead of arguing with him, I took a cigarette, wary of the first puffs, because I hadn't smoked since the day after my father told me I was going to live with Marge and Scofield. Tim talked of his family's poultry business. "This is nothing," he said, and waved a hand at Scofield's crowded kennels. "We have a hundred and fifty thousand birds at any time." He worked for Scofield because at home there was nothing to do. The climate-controlled broiler and layer sheds had automatic feeders, which his mother checked when she looked through the battery cages for dead birds. His father kept the books and cleaned the sheds every few months.

He had cut off the sleeves of his T-shirt, and his soft, threadbare jeans looked as though they hadn't been washed for weeks. While we squatted, sitting on our heels on the worn dirt path around the shed, I wanted to bury my face in the denim of his pants and breathe the smells nestled there, the way I rubbed my nose along the bellies of puppies and into the oily fur behind the ears of dogs. Tim and I rested our arms between our knees and dangled our cigarettes from absent-minded fingers. The more I asked about poultry, the more intent he got on telling me about it, and the more he talked, the more he unknowingly let his soul escape in the breath that filled out his words. Sitting downwind, I secretly breathed him in, kept him talking, and won him over.

"Laying hens are egg-producing machines," he said. "They're rated by their ability to turn the least bit of feed into the most eggs in the shortest time. With the other birds, it's by feed to meat." He had a pimple on his chin and one on his temple, and a month before, I had gotten pimples in the same spots.

The idea of breeding, feeding, and medicating chickens to create ideal grocery products appealed to me because it proved that bodies were just molecules chemically combined. That knowledge was a power that Tim had, and it made the dimples wink in his cheeks as he spoke of the stench of the broiler shed and the sound sixty thousand chickens made when he walked into the shed and they tried to scramble to the far side of their cages, packed nine birds to an eighteen-by-twenty-four-inch space. "It's a big sound," he said, shaking his head to show me I would never believe it. "It's a Niagara, it's a hundred ambulances blaring at once."

I had questions about life cycles, chicken nutrition, incubators, steroids, slaughterhouses. He promised to bring me out to the farm sometime. I listened, both of us interested, as he described debeaking.

Every day he worked we met at lunchtime by the shed. Sometimes, no longer dieting, he brought sandwiches of peanut butter, honey, and grapes bulging between the bread slices, and other times ham, sour cream, and potato chip sandwiches. He called me Sis, and we talked about my parents, his girlfriend Denise, and Mr. Dheil. When he and Denise broke up, I listened to the gradual exposé, slowly realizing that as Tim fumed red-eyed, I was getting calmer and wiser to the point that, even though I was several years behind him in high school, I dominated both his grief and his solace. Finally one afternoon, I was able, through pure beneficence, to make him run crashing through the dead sticks and leaves of the summer woods so we could be alone and I could comfort, disturb, and overawe him with a more adept blow job than Mr. Dheil had ever rifled from me.

~

Marge has gone off to Boston to help plan a large AKC show a few weeks off, to which she plans to take several of her weimaraners. She's buying and selling. She buys and sells dogs so fast Scofield will never understand it. How can you get anything out of them, he says to her, when you don't even have time to see what color they are? She has pups sold before the sire's even wet his prick. Cam has just sidled up the stairs in the TV light, her breasts riding high on her chest just a nick above the banister rail from where he sits. Johnny Carson has finished his monologue, and Scofield likes to fall asleep to the sound of Johnny laughing at his guests, but tonight it'll take a while after seeing her come in from her first date. He hadn't even realized she wasn't in the house, and he scolded her for not telling him she was going out with Timmy. It was just to a movie in town, she said, a PG movie, and Timmy is seventeen and can drive.

"I know how old Tim is," he said, angry at the thought, and he was about to say what does a boy his age want with a little girl when he realized that after all the crap she had been through recently and with a body like that so young, it made sense she'd get along with an older kid.

He is happy her life is falling into normalcy; the attention from other young people is crucial to her, like Marge says, and once she starts school in the fall the phone will ring and ring for her and they will have a beautiful daughter in the house, a young lady. To think of her this way is what he must do, he tells himself; this is the right way to cure the disease of the groin she brought into the house.

While he dozes in front of the TV, he hears a dog's toenails in the kitchen, and at first he thinks nothing of it and remembers old Master, the only dog who lived indoors with them. But old Master died eight years ago and he thinks one of the boys or even Cam let one of the dogs in and he tries to get up to see what's happening but he can't move and David Letterman is grinning gap-toothed at the camera while Paul Shaffer talks on in nonsense. The clicking of a dog's toes ends, and he rests in his body again until he hears the creak of the dining room floorboard, which startles him awake. Letterman is crossing the stage with a man in a lab coat. A dog stands in the archway to the dining room. He knows because, even though all the lights are off, the light from the television hits the walls and bounces off to glint on the wet nose and give a gray sheen to the thick black coat. Letterman acts apprehensive of the table lined with vials of bubbling solutions, and after some banter, the man in the lab coat seriously offers him a vial to drink from. The dog is not a collie like Master, but it has instead the heavy, strong-limbed blackness of a Newfoundland, and he cannot remember the last Newfoundland they owned or boarded. The television audience applauds. He sits up and the dog starts, alarming him, then it wags its tail. He recalls with some real fear the rumors about the wild dogs, formerly his police dogs, and there is, he knows, some truth to it all, and in a moment his mind has the house surrounded—a dog stands firm and staring at each exit and each window as trained, and this one (at least one) has come in to drive him to his death. He listens, and none of his own dogs are barking.

The Newfoundland takes a couple of casual steps forward and looks up the stairs. The solution in the vial turns out to be the flavor banana. Scofield reaches a slow arm up and flicks on the light, and the dog does not flinch or turn, and he wonders for a second if it is blind and then realizes that he can see through it; he sits up on the edge of the couch and grabs both his knees to know that he is awake and the half-visible dog watches him and Scofield's mind bounces with a livid, flipping fear. He jumps to his feet ready to give this dog an overpowering display of his size and aggressiveness, but the dog is entirely at ease. The television tinkles a jingle for a key chain that beeps at the sound of a clap. The Newfoundland starts up the stairs and disappears.

Scofield barrels his torso up the stairs, passing through an icy block of air that catches him in the legs and almost trips him, and bursts into Cam's room, a whirlwind of dirty clothes, magazines, and sheet music. Cam is not there.

〜

Timmy didn't like Harry, and he asked me to stop. We were in the woods at night, at our spot, sitting on Timmy's Mexican blanket with Darcy. Sometimes we snuck a dog out with us, and Tim liked to bring Darcy. We would mostly talk lying down, and Tim would say he wished we could sleep over together and he never mentioned money. Tim grabbed my forearm and squeezed until his chewed-back finger-nails dug in. Darcy watched us closely. I didn't react, because pain is just nerve endings firing, and when you know that, you can feel each nerve pulse like a strobe light or a star. I didn't mind—the nerves fired because Tim was jealous, alive. I explained that I only took Harry in my mouth in the shed during the rainy afternoons next to the rakes and the body bite suits, where we could talk alone and he could lean against the wall and I had room to kneel. I did it to please him as a friend, and never allowed him more. Tim was the only one who reached inside my body with whatever he wanted. Tim got mad. His face screwed up in the dark, and he kept wiping it with his free hand. Then he let me go and punched me in the sternum. Darcy stood up and took Tim's arm in his mouth. Tim told me to take my clothes off, which was okay—we liked to be bare against the bark and damp earth—but he looked at me a long time and said maybe we should cut my body into separate pieces, one for Harry and one for him. I said there were times when that idea made sense to me, and he said the only trouble was Harry would get the smart part and he didn't deserve it. He told me I didn't deserve my smarts either.

〜

"Are you all right?" Cam asks, peeking from behind the bathroom door in her robe. He notices she's wearing makeup.

"Are you?" he says, stepping out of her bedroom. "I thought I heard something."

"The tube," she says, and ducks back into the bathroom, and annoyance couples with his fear of the half-visible Newfoundland and soars. Lately, while she is more settled and less disturbed, she seems to be using what happened between them when she was a kid to develop power over him. At any moment she can make him feel guilty, stupid, perverted. With it, she can drive him and Marge apart, she can take away his standing in the community, pull his wealth out from under him, send him to jail, scoop with one word a canyon between him and his God. Her intention to ruin him stems purely from spite, because what happened ten years ago didn't *really* happen because he never really touched the kid. He had to admit he was carried away and had *wanted* to screw her, but he *didn't do it* and the only *real* thing that happened was that she freaked out and went straight home and told her grandmother, who acted as though he had raped her, turned her parents against him, and did everything short of calling the police. The old woman, it seemed, hadn't told the girl's parents exactly what had happened. At least they never mentioned it, and her father doesn't seem to remember or care. The whole incident has no bearing on Scofield or her, and yet she, out of spite, uses it to undermine him. Maybe something's wrong with her mind, the way her mother had a bolt loose.

He goes back down the stairs, noticing no cold draft, and checks all the doors and window screens, figuring now it was either a real dog or a dream and resisting the impulse to look over his shoulder. He turns off the television, and while he climbs the stairs to bed he gets so depressed and frightened he can hardly move, and he sits down, crushing his weight around himself on the narrow step. He misses Marge, who hardly has time for him, he himself is sometimes too busy even to turn around and take a pee on the lawn though his bladder would like to rip, and the cop stories have been getting to him. The cops come here and work hard, work well with their new dogs, and you know they're going to make an all right team, and then you send them off and get the news. Punks shoot or cut or burn the dogs. They mount a shepherd's head on their wall or sling a dobe's paw on a chain through their belt loop. Even some of the cops flip out and let the dog take a bullet or beat the shit out of it. Scofield swears sometimes that he won't let city cops take his dogs anymore, but the city's where they're needed.

He wonders what he's doing anymore, with his hotshot dogs and his blue-ribbon working wife and the only female who ever got to him, who he ever wanted unforgettably body and soul, asleep right now under his roof, a child who hates him. He rocks himself on the step, and soon he cries big and quiet, lonely for deep arms in the dark to hold him; he longs for confession, not to a priest but to the intimacy of a forgiving body, he yearns to spill himself into acceptance, and he tries to wish that Marge were home, but what he really wants is the nasty, moody little girl with shiny evergreen makeup on her eyelids. He is so tired of wanting her and of repulsing himself, and that's why he's crying.

~

I got uncomfortable the way Tim leaned at me angry across the Mexican blanket with Darcy's gaze bolted on us, his muzzle shut with nervousness. Tim shook down deep inside himself, so I pulled at him and smiled at him with my mouth open nice. Then he fucked me with sweat and bruises. He couldn't come because I disgusted him, he said, and he was huge and hard for so long that he stung and tore me inside. I did everything I had ever learned to excite him enough so that it would end. I stuck my fingers in his bottom, drew my knees up until I thought he would bruise the inside of my spine, made all the sounds of mounting orgasm. About an hour must have passed, and still he pinched my shoulders and heaved his chest over my face, while I grew sickened by the peach-felt plastic of his skin and the gutter of sweat down the middle of his back. Darcy slept a few feet away. Sometimes Tim went soft and I had to work on him. He said, after a while, that his skin was raw, and I had to masturbate to make the fluids run. His elbows bled from the wool blanket, and so did the small of my back. His arms and legs trembled with fatigue. He wouldn't talk to me. All the joints in my hands and hips ached; I grew weak and irritated and said that we could finish tomorrow, and he said, "You make me sick." The half-moon rose over his shoulder, but I could draw no peace from it. The sight of it made me suddenly frantic and I tried to push him off me, but his penis was in me good and I couldn't get it out. He kept pushing it in, and my struggle made him grunt. Darcy lifted his big shepherd's head. I panicked, I said I

had never *wanted* anything or anyone inside me, dividing me, multi-
plying me, segmenting me into portions of pleasure and utility. Mr.
Dheil had murdered and marketed me, had applied money to my
protoplasm. I tore at him, "Get *out!*" I kicked, but he was between
my legs and I had no leverage. The thumping of his metronome hips
continued, and I realized that this was the measure of all my life, the
beat of time passing, its boot-steps on my body; my death. I lay still
and listened to the sound of bone-in-flesh beat against flesh-and-
bone-on-earth. I concentrated on that sound with my eyes closed, so
that I wouldn't see the moon or feel the humiliation ripping up and
down like a cheese grater. Darcy sighed himself back to sleep. I said,
"Try not to come inside me."

"I know."

The rhythm smoothed as I relaxed, and then I hoped he wouldn't
come right away. I imagined what it would be like to come with a
man on me, how my body would open from the pubic bone upward
like a reverse cesarean, my cells opening to swallow his cells; I
thought how Timmy had been jealous, how his jealousy had made
him hurt me, how he had sat with me at lunchtime and in the woods
many nights, investing his time, hugging me and listening to me
unravel my entrails of loneliness. I thought maybe he had wanted to
contain them. Maybe he wanted to negate them. If I let Harry have
my mouth, then his come would line my entrails and Tim would have
to contain both me and Harry. Maybe Tim wanted just me because
he really thought I was smart and pretty and good—the things he said
to make me take my jeans off. Thinking that maybe he sincerely liked
me, I wanted my body to unseam itself beneath him so that I could be
the things he said I was and only them and not just undressed. I
wanted it, wanted it wanted wanted. He pulled out and I snapped my
hand around his penis.

I turned my face to the prickly blanket and let him scrape his come
off me with leaves. Darcy stood up and shook himself off. I was
feverish with disappointment, weak in every bone. "Get up," he said,
stepping into his pants, his bare toes balancing him on the blanket.

"I'm sick," I said, and when I heard my voice I knew I was sick. It
felt like dizzy fever, probably from some moss-borne virus.

"You're the sickest girl I know," he said.

My eyes bled something hot down my face, out of my nose, into
the blanket, weeping into the mud. Every feeble movement squeezed
leakage from my eyes, and my mind turned inward, pirouetting

toward some dark, quiet brink where there was no moon. He was saying he was sorry. He held me and helped me get dressed. A brother. He helped me walk. When I walked I felt better, but my pants hurt me. My mind kept lifting itself to the top of my skull. I imagined my mind might seep up through the seams, and my mother and I and Grandmom would know together the secrets of bodilessness. Darcy trotted ahead.

There is no heaven.

"I can't see you anymore," Tim said as we put Darcy back in his kennel.

I said I knew. I spun around and hugged him as though I was irresistibly affectionate, and I clung to him, smelled his sweat and heat and faint sex, clung not to his company or his approval of my attractiveness but to the keenness of blighted hope. "Can you be my brother again, without touching me?"

He was anxious to leave; I knew it before I asked, and knew the answer no matter what he said. I felt my arms around the answer in his stance, in his long pause; I could hear it in his breath. "Sure. I could try." He gave me a quick squeeze and let me go. "Better get to bed," my brother said, my brother anxious to leave so he could come back to work the next day and ignore me.

~

He slowly hauls himself up the rest of the flight, afraid again of the half-visible dog, of the madness of that vision. The desire for the girl is mundane, he knows. It's normal for a middle-aged man to ache to recapture youth by seizing its skin. It's normal to find the forbidden titillating, and if only he had not sipped it ten years ago he would not know now how intoxicating it is. He stands outside her door bordered in blackness and knows she is sleeping in her long T-shirt, in her fading grief for her dead mother, in vague anticipation of young adulthood. He is torn between the urge to join her in her bed, embrace her like a needy, humiliated, repentant lover, and the urge to kneel outside her door, sob freely and jerk off. Both degrade him and betray his weakness. He tries to talk himself into having a beer, picking up a *Playboy,* calling a friend, even shooting himself. He thinks of paperwork that needs to be done, dog toenails to be clipped. He tries to hate Cam, and this is easy and it only gives him such a hard-on that he opens his pants, rubs himself, and hates her. He faces himself now, a prisoner with two choices: he can kneel down and do groveling homage to his forbidden idol, or he can rape her and love her and begin a life of terrible freedom. In the air his bare cock prickles and aches and he steps toward her door, only a shoulder of cold air leans against his legs and he stops. His penis softens as his concentration shifts to the loose skin of his throat, exposed. A fog must be sliding by, but August fog is not this cold. It feels as though a freezer door stands open, spilling its cascade and river of cold, but nothing explains how fog or cold has risen to the second floor. It's his fear, his insanity chilling him; mid-life crisis impels him to damage his marriage, his canine empire, his peace of mind. The skin and muscle of his belly hurts him from bouncing it hard when he ran up the steps earlier. He tucks in his cock and closes his pants, almost laughing. He tries to lose himself in the comfort of assuming responsibility for the temperature, and he shuts the second-floor windows, even the one in Cam's room. She sleeps unseen but for the rise of her blanketed hip under the thin window light. When Scofield pulls the window shut, she says "What," and he feels nothing more for her than pissed at his cousin for unloading her there.

～

Marge stood in the bedroom doorway watching her husband. When he leaned into the light of his desk lamp with his glasses on and his eyes squinting even behind the expensive lenses, she loved him. The thing that keeps you married is light, she thought. If it weren't for different qualities of light and different angles, by this time she would be sick of his puffy jowls and his dark brown eye sockets. If the shadow of his beard didn't darken the swing of his throat, she would have left him by now. Time kept you together too; smashed into fragments and evenly spaced in various places with different angles of light. She would do more with light. She would buy candles and three-way bulbs for each room. She would get him to come to dog shows with her more often, sleep with her in the camper. Unless he lost weight, though, he was stagnant in any light in any place. If he lost weight, he would be different in space, and the light that struck him would vary.

"Cam's not here," she said. Scofield did not look up. "Again," she said.

"It's my fault," he said, his face, with his glasses on, a different array of lines and his eye sockets almost white.

"Responsible for everything and yet you do nothing." She saw how the dogs affected them, how Scofield sat in his flesh folds like a bloodhound, his eyes averted while she, standing still, drove at him for a response. "You know what could be happening." Since Cam had come, fragmenting their private time, fragmenting the house, forcing out the possibility of candles and three-way bulbs, he had been aching. Without touching Marge, he hung on her, pulled at her arms, lay dead bulllike in front of her feet. She felt him all day long, while she walked figure Ts and performed stands-for-examination, taxing her body's very frame while she had coffee on the road with Ritter.

"It's my fault," he said, and turned his nose toward her a fraction, the glasses on his face suddenly absurd, like boxer shorts on a cat. "But never mind."

~

Scofield has seen the half-visible dog several times in the last few weeks. He stopped dozing before the TV, believing the dog a part of half-sleep, but then he saw it cross the lawn in broad daylight while he dug a hole for a willow sapling.

One night as he did his books at the kitchen table, he saw it make its way mildly over the brightly lit linoleum, through the dark dining room, and out into the light of the stairwell, and he dashed outside and jogged over the moonless lawn to the first kennel. He grabbed Marge's weim Deputy by the nape of his long, dust-haired neck and jogged him into the house. Deputy rattled splay-legged through the kitchen, and in the blackness, galloped around the dining room table, then stopped. Scofield watched from the kitchen, fascinated, as the dog cried out once, his eyes, clearly in the dark, stunned with puzzlement. He bristled and cringed, a brave young dog for the first time afraid. The Newfoundland stood at the foot of the stairs; its great head rose like soot hanging in the air, and it looked up to the top of the flight, as though unconscious of its audience, unconscious that it was massively immaterial, that the sight of it held more awe than the healing hands of prophets. Deputy leapt at the Newfoundland with hesitation, as though doubting both his eyes and his sanity.

The Newfoundland reacted—braced itself and met the assault. They spun together and rose one above the other, their noses to the ceiling, the bone and gristle of their mouths flashing. Then Deputy sank struggling to the floor, pinned with his lips yanked back, pinned by nothing. He screamed. Scofield ran to him without thinking, and the mattress of cold lay all around him.

"What the hell's going on down there?" Marge called from upstairs.

"Nothing, damn it. It's just me." Deputy burst from under his hands and crashed backward into the coffee table.

"Jesus!" Marge said.

"Go back to bed, God damn it! I'll be right up."

"Lovely." Marge's footsteps made their way to the bedroom above.

Deputy leaned back against the toppled coffee table, the sharp bird cage of his ribs strained above his lungs, his muzzle a narrow protean grimace—terror, anger, submission—his eyes blindly crazed.

～

"Be a good little niece and take your bath," he says. He imagines the heavy water hammers into the deep porcelain tub. He sees himself kneel on the warped linoleum and hug a tiny, preschool Cam.

"I'm too sleepy," she says. He stands her on the vanity and undresses her, brushes out her wispy babylike hair while she totters, falling asleep on her feet. He lowers her sound asleep into the steaming water, where she floats, a tiny body nestled in the water-velvet of the giant white coffin. He lies down naked on her and she sinks peacefully to the bottom, and the hot water envelopes their bodies, joined in the fiercest grip. With his head above the splashing, he watches her face sleeping beneath the froth.

～

Tonight Marge is at her mother's for the night, Cam is up in her room playing her flute, and Scofield phones Father Tom, the only priest in the diocese interested in such matters.

"No one else has seen it but me, far as I know," Scofield says again. He sits on the couch facing the stairwell, and above him Cam's music is loud, erratic; she plays the same few notes over and over, getting them right.

Scofield struggles with an urge for a cigarette, although he is not a smoker. He wants something to do with his hands, he figures, because Father doesn't believe him. He leans over to the coffee table to fold the corners of the paper napkin up around the sides of his beer glass.

"I don't know how many nights I'm going to have to have you or someone else reliable sit here to prove it," Scofield says.

"I don't know what to tell you," Father says, "If it's anything at all, it's a barghest—a dog ghost—and it's harmless."

"It almost killed my dog. You think I'm a fool?" Scofield gets up and tries to pace the short length of the phone cord. He feels like screaming at Cam to stop the goddamn noise, but he can't with a priest on the phone. "Get rid of it. Exorcise it. Throw a bead at it." Scofield takes the last gulp of warm beer.

He sits down and wraps one arm over the back of the couch. Now that he knows there's a name for it, the dog ghost doesn't amaze him; it's ordinary—it's an object outside the question of his sanity, and he's sick of it. The priest explains that he's read about animal ghosts. A barghest is not a demonic possession; it involves no evil. The church believes animals have souls—lesser souls—and that any spirit can draw energy from human distress, enough to make the spirit visible to human eyes.

Scofield shakes his knees back and forth rapidly, to keep himself alert. Cam's overture drums at his tolerance, tangling with the priest's obliging information, striking him toward sleep.

The priest goes on about how records show that spirits of dogs often appear near disturbed pubescent girls, and Scofield realizes he never could pay attention when a priest spoke, and he counts the beers he swallowed before he called Father; he recognizes he feels threatened by this forty-year-old youngster eager to teach him about the spirit world. Dog-spirits—barghests—are thought by some to foretell misfortune, Father Tom says, but studies done by the church have shown them to be associated with strong human emotions. An abandoned house may be haunted simply because of the energy that frightened passersby impart.

"So I get rid of Cam and the dog leaves." Scofield, alarmed, feels his consciousness about to clap shut, asleep.

"Well, there's a nun in this parish who's a counselor she could see."

Scofield can't believe he called this man. Not that the guy isn't reasonable and reputably well informed in a controlled, conservative way, but he's from out of town and a priest. The man hasn't blessed him once. Apparently, this isn't a religious issue. Maybe nothing is anymore. The analyst replaces the medium. Group therapy replaces exorcism. There is no good or evil, simply "energy." But even though the man is nothing right now but a dissociated voice, Scofield is conscious of his priestliness, has been since the first two times they met years ago at K. of C. meetings, and knowing Father Tom is a priest—a professional confessor, a seeker of confessees—Scofield has even gone so far as to invite him to his home to watch his nightmare like a rented movie. He wonders about himself now, while the priest explains how therapy will ease the very recesses of Cam's troubled mind; when he called him was he looking for an exorcist, or looking unconsciously for a confessor, someone to forgive him?

"Cammie doesn't need any of this crap." The effort of speech tilts his head backward. The priest does not reply, and he thinks maybe the psychoanalysis was meant for him. The strange man has hypnotized him over the phone. Confession capers before him, a catnip mouse on a string.

～

Sick and scared and feeling voluminous pity for myself, I did not bother being quiet as I came in. The kitchen was silver and black. My nose ran, and I sucked the mucus over my upper lip. In the dining room, acres of dizzying darkness, I took off my pants and cupped myself with my hand. In the spanking yellow light of the bathroom, my urine stung me, the toilet paper stuck to me and peeled off with faint streaks of red. My face put out its salty wetness, and my nose blew bubbles as I breathed. I wiped it with a towel and threw it in the hamper. My mind bumped against the roof of my skull, a tired grackle trapped in a barn.

With just my shirt on, I knelt on my bed and looked out the window. From there I could see the bank of forest into which Tim and I had gone to share bodies and talk. Tim simply couldn't handle being a body-sharer and a friend, the way Mr. Dheil could. The moon stood stark over the tree tops, a half-moon pointing downward, the giant white-hot tip of an iron penis. The image amused me and cleared my mind, so I tried another, something about a kneecap, but couldn't think about bodies at all. I seemed to have used up all the chemicals my brain needed to form body-thoughts. All I could think about was the shape and whiteness of the moon's turned-aside featureless face, the universe its color-empty cloak, draping me. I wondered if I wanted to die, which made me try to remember my mother's perfume and the smell of our old house, and with that I used up all the brain-chemicals needed for material thoughts; somehow I felt small and childish. Water rose in my eyes, and I watched the moon sink in it.

Someone was in the room behind me; the air changed against the backs of my legs, and my eyes focused on the screen in the window before my face. All the tired muscles under my skin came alive with tension. I held my breath and listened hard and heard nothing, so after a few minutes I tried to forget it, but my whole being was convinced. I heard nothing and did not relax but wound my flesh tighter around my bones until, deaf and blind and brainless, I heard within the hollows of my mind's ear, "I love you, little one."

~

"Be a good niece and take your bath," Scofield says. "I'm going to stand right here and make sure you do it." Against the gold and orange flowered wallpaper of his mind she leans, and looks up at him to see if he's serious. When she sees that he is, she pulls off her sweatshirt with a smile. She's only about ten, but already her nipples are supple swells on her lanky torso. She holds still with her eyes closed, stifling giggles while he puts makeup on her face. He feels a sharp knot of shit in his bowels, and won't let himself touch her until they're both naked and he's sitting on the toilet. Then she sits on his lap, and when he shits he comes at the same time.

He sits drinking coffee in the kitchen with Marge, and Cam walks in naked and dazed. "I'm bleeding," she says, and holds her palms out wide, smeared with blood, and maroon liquid streams down her legs and snakes in impossibly animated rivulets across the floor.

~

When I was four and five, my mother shut the door behind me at seven-thirty in the morning, and if I looked back through the foggy living room curtains, I could see her heavily climb the stairs in her silk and lace nightie, on her way back to bed. Grandmom pulled up in her Chevy, and I crossed the lawn and got in next to her. I buckled up, and then she pulled away from our house, a house of shadows, perfume, and sweat.

Grandmom reminded me every morning, so that I could never forget, to pray for my brothers and sisters, my half-brothers and half-sisters, whom my mother refused to birth. Grandmom never said how many there were. "There are things people must forget. I'm helping you forget." She taught me to hide my prayers and my sibling-thoughts from my parents, who were trying to forget, even though my siblings occupied me. I imagined that an abortion meant the baby never came out, but the soul left the body, now one of several abandoned bodies crowded in my mother's belly like a hefty litter of dead kittens, and the souls hovered about her, hung in her hair, pulling it straight, plucked and tugged at her breasts. I felt near to them when near her; I had slept a fetus pressed among their bodies; when born I was torn from them. My mother, who had the power of life and death, who could have given many life and chose not to, had given life to me, and according to the laws of probability, the fact that it was me and not some other soul allowed to live made perfect sense only in that it was entirely arbitrary. My life was due to luck and my mother's will. I had escaped the spite and magic of Medea. The only survivor, the only child who ever breathed at all, I wondered if the others weren't worthier somehow—because they were sacrificed, they were extraordinary.

One brother in particular took to me. Michael left my mother and draped himself all around my skin like a gown. When I was very young, I couldn't fix his features in my mind, but he was always leaning his sadness on my arms because I prayed for him. I prayed for him alone because I couldn't pray for something I couldn't count, something that was to me as innumerable as a war. At night I lay on my back so he could put his vacuous fingers in my mouth and dig at my eyes, and I sometimes wished he could just suck my life through my nostrils. And as I learned about boys and husbands and boy-friends—companions for older girls—I could picture him. He had short, thick brown hair and a skinny body and long, thin legs, like Mom and me. He was my twin, my intimate. He slept on top of me when I slept, to blanket me from all the otherness I couldn't see. By the time Mr. Dheil had my promise of secrecy and had blanketed me with things I could see, Michael was leaving me anyway. I got tired of his half-presence, which he couldn't help.

At church Grandmom and I sat up near the altar, by the candles burning in fat red glass holders. Before Father Robert started Mass, Grandmom said her rosary, her lips shaping and rapidly sucking backward the syllables of God. Father Robert knelt on the other side of the church and looked at me over his shoulder, which I hated because it broke my concentration on Michael and the candles. Grandmom said the lighted glasses were "special intentions"; inside them burned candles, which sent a ribbon of prayer-smoke forever heavenward. When God smelled them, He blessed the person prayed for. One candle was mine, she said. I didn't see candles in red glass, though. I saw squat, wide-eyed red owls, elfin owls, burning with their own thoughts, sending up their own prayers, owls spiteful and mischievous who needed to be won over. While at the altar Father spoke and broke Christ in two, I tried to make the candles like me. My goal was to have them all praying for us, not just the one. I told them about my afternoons, about my Playschool farmhouse and my Lego sets. I told them that Grandmom said we needed their smoke prayers, that I had to pray for others or I would remember my own sin and would not be innocent, that Mom had to forget she had killed so she could stop killing. They blinked and turned their heads around. I tried to guess which lighted one was mine, but every day they changed places with the unlit ones.

~

"Well, I guess Mom's with all her dead babies by now," I said. Dad and I were driving to the grocery store, and I said it because I couldn't stand him being so handsome and clumsy but unconquerable, even though he had just put his wife in the ground. It was our first grocery store trip as a family of two, and I knew he didn't have a list.

His lips bulged and flexed over his teeth. He looked from me to the road back and forth so quickly I thought he was about to hit me. "Who the *fuck* . . . told you that?" The passenger-side wheels slammed over the gravel on the shoulder, and he pulled the car back on the road. "Your God. Damned. Grandmother."

When we got to the store, he parked with a jolt and scrambled out of the car. I followed him and watched him walk with his neck hunched and his legs long-striding, his hands plunged in his pants pockets and his suit-jacket fronts flapping behind him. I stopped. At the hospital he had hugged me and had spoken to doctors and signed papers dry-eyed. At the funeral he wiped away tears of uprootedness and indecision. I had shaken him; he was mine. He grabbed a cart and swung it, grinding on the edges of its rickety wheels, toward the electric-eye door, then shoved it into the wall. He walked back toward me. "Get in the car," he said.

In the car, in the Shop'N'Bag parking lot, he told me my mother had run away pregnant as a teenager and had an abortion. He just talked, without asking me how much I already knew. When they married, she was irresponsible with birth control and had an aborted pregnancy without telling him. Once she fell sick, and he caught her eating a houseplant, trying to poison herself. In the hospital, they found out she was pregnant. Then Dad and she moved to town to be near Grandmom, who was to watch over us.

I said, so, Mom tried to kill me?

"Not you, but the idea of giving birth. The idea of having her life altered."

I asked, what about after me?

"We both got lazy," he said to the windshield.

～

At the dog show, Marge leaned on her grooming table, her cheeks aching from smiling all day, and watched Ritter's Airedale pup refuse to stand for examination, wheeling and crouching to put its rump safely on the ground. Ritter glanced up at her, exasperated, with his left hand hooked between the dog's back legs. The judge stepped in front of him, and Marge gave her cheeks a rest. She squatted down by Deputy's crate and twined her fingers through the bars for him to lick. Once she and the dogs had driven off in the camper, the dog settled down and did well in show. In the obedience class novice he only took third, but Marge had expected that anyway. In her world of paw prints and dog ammonia, everything was fine, but Marge worried about herself. She had outfitted the camper with a Saturday night dinner for two. She remembered thinking maybe she'd invite Ritter over, Ritter who had shared coffee and shop talk with her for the last three years. When Marge fixed herself breakfast in the morning and saw the pork chops, she knew she wanted to be alone that night in her camper, with him.

"Eleven—isn't that a stupid number?" he said when she asked how many kids he had when they first met three years ago. He fathered four by his first wife and seven by his second, and now he didn't live with either.

"Not stupid, just odd," she said, and he thought she had made a joke.

He came to dog shows with none of the handler's usual equipment. His champion bitch, Otley, was simply tied by her obedience lead to the bar of an emergency exit. When Otley saw Ritter returning, she stood up and plopped a paw into her water bowl. Marge had never much cared for terriers. They came through the K-9 City school occasionally—the Kerry blue, the Airedale, and of course the bull. But a terrier was too trim and cunning for true obedience, too likely to question your authority no matter how you overpowered it.

A little bored, Marge stepped over to Otley, who greeted her with the polite nose-in-the-hand shake. Young, leggy, strong, and square, Otley had a strange, power-packed grace, not a Doberman's unconscious elegance, but a deliberate control. Marge knelt, and Otley offered her the dry paw. Marge scratched Otley's chest, and the bitch's face was serene amid the odors of hot dogs and doughnuts, urine and fear, and the clamor of hundreds of shoes and paw pads. A shivering miniature poodle, shaved and coiffured, wailed in a nearby crate. Otley's beard was mussed, flattened at the chin from sleep and fuzzed around the muzzle, giving her a kind of cartoon face. She stretched her muscled neck toward Marge, gently, her eyes so direct they startled. Otley paused. Her throat worked—a swallow. Her tongue, a bright pink petal of velvet, trembled between the gleam of her teeth. The soft black nose bumped Marge's as the tongue licked over her lips. For a second Marge wondered if the dog tasted her lipstick, and was sorry she'd worn it.

Ritter said he realized in the ring that Otley's puppy, Ben, just had too much giddiness in him to be any value in show. Otley and Ben wiggled and licked each other's faces. Ben jumped on Marge as she knelt there, nearly knocking her over sideways.

"So work with him extra." Marge ruffled Ben's scissor-sculpted ears; then he bounced to the end of his lead and wheezed with strangulation.

"He's just stupid, Marge." Ritter, openly disappointed, seemed ready to hang the dog by his leash. "Watch this. Heel," he said dejectedly, and hauled his seemingly deaf dog away from the miniature poodle, whose terrified eyes bulged like white chicken eggs.

The voice on the loudspeaker, which she had listened to for seven hours straight without noticing, suddenly pealed in her ears. It set off in her mind Cam's blood-boiling overture, which now pranced like a goat, bruising her thoughts. She resented Ritter exhaustively and wished he would leave, but she knew if he took one step away she would seize him by his silly T-shirt. Insanity had never touched her or anyone in her family, yet she felt she lived on the edge of it. It could blow down all the platforms of logic she walked upon, snip off and cauterize her hopes, and worst of all, squelch any self-recognition, so that she'd believe she had nothing to regain.

~

My mother played a game with me, a spontaneous game only she ever knew the rules to. I came upon her, say, as she watched TV in the guest room with a book on her lap. "What are you reading, Mommy? What are you watching?"

She pretended not to hear me.

I tapped her on the sleeve of her ivory robe.

"How did you get in the house?" she said, alarmed. "Who are you?"

I explained that I was her daughter, she knew that.

"I know nothing of the kind. I have no children." Baby souls, wafted from her womb, clung to her robe from collar to hem, and some in her hair, some crushed between her body and the green chair, all of them staring at me, fiercely pouting.

I gripped the arm of the chair and shook myself back and forth. "Come o-o-o-on!"

"Whose little girl are you? You're cute." She asked my name and address.

I recited them and added, "I live with Daddy and *you,* Mommy." I went to poke her when I said "*you,*" but feared poking one of the little images stuck to her robe.

"I'm Mrs. Finkelmeyer and I've never seen you before in my life. Tell you what. You can have lunch here, but then you're going to have to leave."

It was obviously a game, but I never knew when it would end. I saw myself living in the bushes until Daddy got home. And what if he didn't know me either? At some point, I always started to cry.

In the kitchen, she asked what I wanted to eat.

"What do you have?" I said, slyly playing along. She told me her menu, and I picked something. While I ate, she asked me questions about what I did with my days and how I liked the thought of school. The little spirits, eternally silent, made the gestures of sniffling and kicked about, getting agitated, holding their breath, their faces clenched like fists. Mrs. Finkelmeyer watched me closely.

I told her I was looking forward to school, because I'd be away from my mother. "I know I shouldn't say this," I said, "but she isn't very nice to me."

"Oh, I'm sorry to hear that." Mrs. Finkelmeyer reached to pat my arm, dragging a little bluish body across the Formica.

I hated her. I kicked the leg of the table hard, and milk leapt out of my glass.

"All finished?" She pulled the plate away with half of my peanut butter sandwich on it.

She stood up smiling, warmly amused, and the faces opened wide all over her robe, screaming and screaming, clutching feebly at the ivory fabric, their little arms tired of hanging on. Some of them fell off and exploded like soap bubbles on the floor.

"Stop it right now!" she shouted and grabbed my arms as I swung at her. She gripped me, pressing me against the dead bodies, which I struck with my fists because they were sucking their thumbs and trying to stroke my skin. "Hold still," she said. Drained and head-achy, I breathed the patchouli on her neck, and relaxed. "That's my girl," she said, and I drew back to look her in the face.

"Where've you been?" She tickled me. "I've been looking all over for you."

~

People and dogs shuffled past the spot where Marge sat right on the floor in her denim skirt, Scofield's weight linked to her bones. With her arm around Otley's back, she dully watched strangers file with their dogs in and out of the ring beneath the voices of the loudspeaker, which circled them all like buzzards. Ritter stood beside her, squinting as though into bright light although the arena was dimly lit. "I love Otley," Marge said loudly, so he could hear her over the racket. As soon as she said it, the intrigue the dog held for her vanished. If she had really loved Airedales, she would have bought herself one, and had she done that, she wouldn't have had as much reason to look forward to seeing Otley; she would have had to admit she really looked forward to seeing Ritter. Her bones lightened; she got up and started to sweep the hair clippings from the grooved plastic pad of her grooming table. A woman whose name she couldn't remember stopped to chat, her pug, a muscular troll of a dog, curled in her arms.

When the woman left, Marge asked if Ritter had any more of Otley's puppies. With her fingertips she massaged her cheeks, sore from so much smiling. "I want one for Cam." She felt she was recovering from a brief but very bad cold.

"Can you stand this one?" He held out Ben's lead. "Here." Ben, with his back to them, sat on one hip, watching a keeshond jump with a dumbbell in its mouth.

Marge objected. That was a valuable dog, she said.

"He bugs me, Marge." Ritter held out the lead, and she took it. "Try him out. We'll talk about papers later."

He said he'd take her out to a steak house for dinner, and she didn't mention her pork chops. She had to hang around until the end of the show. Her weimaraner Crystal had won Best of Breed and had to compete for Best of Winners.

Suddenly irritated, she said, "Where will he sleep tonight?" and held the lead in her hand up high.

～

When the voice said, "I love you, little one," I felt peace, not just because I wasn't threatened, but because the voice had come from inside my head, a most intimate contact, undeniable, infinitely private, brief. It was perhaps the voice of my brother Michael, come to steal my breath again, or the voice of my mother, visiting me from not-life to reassure me that she wanted a child after all, and not just any child, but me, and she loved that I could play music, and if she would only say again that she loved me I would be free of all bodies, especially Mr. Dheil's, because sharing bodies affirms the right to live, a right I wouldn't need if she were to come from the dead and whisper again, so I could be sure, "Little one." Yet somehow I knew it wasn't my mother, but some inner voice, some meek spirit possessing me.

After the voice left, I was lonely again, but felt like taking good care of myself. I put Vaseline on the lips of my vagina to ease the burning. With my favorite flannel pajamas on, I made myself a Swiss cheese sandwich. Uncle Scofield staggered into the kitchen, blinking in the light, to ask me what the hell I was up to. Feeling gracious, I offered to make him a sandwich, even though I hated the shelf of his belly visible through his half-open robe, his messy beard and hair, the gumminess around the bridge of his eyeglasses. He insisted I eat at the kitchen table rather than in my room, and then he went back to bed.

From the kitchen window I could see the moonlit grass and the shadows of dogs as they slept or paced in the kennels. The mind—the soul—I thought, could not be a mere biochemical symphony of synapses. Who conducted the mind as it puzzled or slept? Was it like random parakeet garble, parakeets who change their music according to what they see and hear—a sudden shadow, a jet of water, the whistle of a finch? My thoughts idled; the answers didn't seem to matter. Intuition told mankind over continents and centuries that the mind and body could be separated, were separated permanently at death. Life overlapped with spatial objects; it was something other, not something equal. Sleep and death testified to this. Many spirits at the moment of their death appeared to distant relatives who knew nothing of their last breaths—this was a fact, a widely known, inexplicable fact. I believed the caged dogs would pace forever in the moonlight, breathing through their black-snouted muzzles, thinking their dog-thoughts, because the essence of their minds—the unity of their synaptic symphonies—must make some sort of impression on space. Most of reality is an invisible soup of somnambulant repetition, disembodied souls going through the motions of their whole lives in every second. My own past selves kicked angrily at the footrest of a new highchair, braided a girlfriend's hair on a school bus, massaged the loose, wrinkled skin of Mr. Dheil's back. My mother forever climbed the stairs in her satin nightgown.

But I wondered about creatures of the imagination. If I pictured Darcy escaping from his confines, trotting to the house, where I met him at the back door, and taking, with gentle teeth, a piece of cheese from my fingers, would that too make an eternal imprint on space? Suppose instead I pictured a dog I had never seen before, a shaggy white one, and gave it a piece of my sandwich. If this dog forever crossed the lawn, that meant that space was full not only of imagined people and situations, but of dream cars and dragons, children never born and unicorns, enchanted islands and time machines. Dragons painted or written about multiplied for every viewer and reader. Hitler had millions of faces, all the same, and he died millions of violent, vengeful deaths. Christ masturbated many times simply because many people wondered. Fame immortalized exponentially. However, unlike ghosts, creatures of the imagination were not known to overlap space, momentarily making themselves visible to the startled human eye. There were, as far as I knew, no baffling but meticulously researched and documented cases of spectral centaurs strutting on patios. Creations of the mind had existence and eternity only insofar as art and humans did. Likewise our being, then, was dependent upon some oversoul. Maybe I believed in God.

～

Scofield damns Marge in the kitchen for bringing home another dog. "We keep buying and breeding and not selling," he says. "Are you nuts?" They have two litters of pups due. They need to advertise in more papers. Marge says she has six deposits on the shepherd pups and only feels five in the bitch's belly. She's got two deposits on the Bouviers, and always sells them at shows if not to cops. She yells at Scofield for not noticing the new dog. "You were around all day and didn't see it. The dogs know; they paid attention," she says. "I could have a lover in the house for a week before you'd holler."

"Same here," he says. "At least I'm home." He leaves and slams the screen door.

"Do you want me to sell dogs or not?" she calls after him.

He walks away backward. "They're standing in their own shit as it is, and you bring home an Airedale." He slaps both hands on his head, still walking backward. He points at Cam, who kneels on the grass before Ben, stretched out on his back with four paws in the air, and she combs the puppy hair that still dusts his belly. "You could have given her a Bouvier. I'd give her Darcy. Cam! Darcy's yours." He points at Marge's shape, blurred and lead-colored through the screen.

He turns and continues, stumbling as he glances at his watch. The growl of a car on the front gravel drive dissolves in the howls of at least sixty-five dogs. "Why aren't you at school?" he says to Cam.

"Took the day to play with my baby," she says, and draws the comb through the light wire hair on his ribs. The dog, still on his back, stiffens, and his polished black eyes follow Scofield's face. For a second, Scofield wonders what spell she casts to keep a dog from joining in the ruckus, but then remembers the dog is too new to feel territorial. The dog's genitals lie great between his thighs like a ginger root.

"Who do you think you are, young lady?"

"It's Columbus Day," she says slowly, through a creeping grin. "No school."

Embarrassment tires him out fast. "Don't get smart," he says, but can't make his words mean anything. He pulls his pants up a little higher and concentrates all his pride into one puzzled look meant to make her doubt she's even worth her weight in sand. Officer Phelan rounds the path by the house with his shepherd. The kenneled dogs reach a higher pitch, and the bloodhounds do chords.

Cam and her dog stand up abruptly. "Uncle Scofield?" she says, but he's greeting Phelan and doesn't answer, explaining they'll be ready in fifteen minutes, go on the long way around the kennels.

Her dog stands beside her, no collar, no leash—to him, a serious offense. "Are you crazy?" he says to her. "All summer long I taught you this business. Without a leash, he'll end up flattened in the road, or worse he'll get in a fight with George there and you'll be picking fur out of the trees."

"Hair. Airedales have hair," she says. "Can he be a house dog?" She loops a choke chain over the dog's head.

"We haven't had a house dog in almost ten years," he says, adjusting the collar to the proper position on the neck. The dog stands for him, and stops panting and watches until he walks away. He speaks into his headset to ask the man who plays decoy to give them fifteen minutes, and he thinks it would be nice for the girl to have her dog with her at night, but then remembers the Newfoundland. He whirls around. "Absolutely not," he says, but Cam has her Airedale off in the sun in the side yard, walking in a zigzagging *heel*.

◞

In symphonic band tryouts I got one of the best chairs, passing most of the upperclassmen. Since I knew few people, I got few congratulations, and Aunt Marge and Uncle Scofield had little idea what an accomplishment third chair was for a freshman. The director urged us all to practice an hour a day in addition to our daily rehearsals together. I scoffed. What did the other musicians do with their time, I wondered, when I spent up to four hours a day going over music I had already played several hundred times? Sometimes, absorbed, I played late into the night, just fingering the keys on my lap and blowing into the air, threading my thoughts through timing and cadence, turns and arpeggios, without the encumbrance of sound. But sound was power, and every afternoon I occupied the Scofield household with *The Planets* or "Song without Words." Accompanied only by the driving memory of the one-hundred-twenty-piece band's rehearsal, my mind snuffed out the chug of the dishwasher and the whir of the air conditioners, even as I counted a thirty-two bar rest. Mine were hours of plunder, marching through the molecules of tables, pictures, wallpaper, figurines, stripping them of all their representational value, their sentimental, aesthetic, or functional purpose, flushing consciousness into the musical void.

Once a week we had flute lessons during school. The two girls who sat in the first and second chairs and I met with the band director. The only things that gave me more pleasure than these lessons were the moments during rehearsals with the entire band when we synchronized pitch, timing, and expression with near excellence, when our souls rode with the momentum created by our eyes, breath, and hands, a carousel of vibrating air. When the music ended, a hundred and twenty people caught each other's eyes with short-winded smiles, then clapped and whooped. In contrast, I liked the lessons with the two girls because they heightened my aloneness. Older and more musically experienced, they fueled my keenness for perfected skill. The director, Mr. Dombrowski, barreled us through harmonic and melodic scales, forced us to gulp down finger exercises, and kept the four of us, while sitting knee to knee, so well vaulted in abstraction as to nullify the possibility of sex between him and any one of us.

Mr. Dheil had driven me to improve my music by making me fear his disappointment. Lessons passed in which I didn't even open my flute case, but he could tell how profitable my practices had been by my self-confidence. If I didn't hesitate to climb naked on his body or didn't flinch under his gaze and fingertips, it was because I had successfully managed all the key changes in "Gypsy Rondo." If, instead of delaying his orgasm with creative tantalizers, I faithlessly worked on him with rapid contact, watching the clock, it was because I had overblown the low notes during the pianissimo of Sonata no. 5.

Free of him, music got better. Music had, I learned, nothing to do with sharing bodies. When I played my favorite overture, the effect it had on listeners was irrelevant, and so was any judgment they had of my skill. The only people who mattered in the pomp of sound were Caesar Giovannini and I, united aloft space and time by his mind printed on sheet music and mine not shaking in the air but losing itself in his anomalous arrangements of nothingness *Allegro*, he said, and my flute lifted to my mouth, *con spirito*.

/ t / w / o /

viruses

When I realized that heaven was null and physicality was wretched, and that the only unions worth living for were those of pure non-corporeality, I sought them constantly in music, which joined me to Holst in a grand, frightening rhapsody; the throat of my soul relaxed and stretched to swallow him whole. Reading was the same. I discovered in English class that I could spray my mind into the mist of Hamlet's, so as to be one with a non- and never-existent being and also one with Shakespeare, penetrated by so many millions over the centuries that reading him—a necrophilic whoring—gave me a stale, decadent thrill. I wanted a realm neither living nor nonliving, neither mortal nor immortal, in which my mind could achieve something other than its death. In literature or in music, no one took from me or disappointed me. There, I forgot that I would die. It was there, I hoped, that the soul goes after life to look for the heaven that isn't. I sat alone, light-headed from hunger, on the dark hall floor, with the memory of Mars, the Bringer of War, advancing—a slow march of ragged soldier spirits on the wet air of night, a rhythmic crashing through dead branches, rising and spinning to the cloud of unknowing. By smelling my mother's torn and temporary shroud and by concentrating on words in the hurtle of nonsound, I studied, a scholar of loss, all I could about my mother, mostly through images of her— the seams of her gray suit and the gold stickpin, a *K* in the lapel, the thin nest of fur her cat, Folly, left on the bedspread, the huge grass mat on the kitchen floor, its joints broken and rotten from footsteps and dampness. Everything stank of patchouli.

I walked without sound into her dark bedroom, avoiding the sight of her bed, my eyes fixed on the dresser. A three-inch-high perfume bottle sat on a lace doily Grandmom had made. The tiny white loops and knots of thread were stained with orange-brown spots, dripped from the glass stopper of the bottle. Except for the neck and base, the blown-glass bottle had the shape of a perfect skipping stone, a smooth, flat oval in the palm of the hand. The glass was a blend of smoky iridescence, black, pink, and green rising, spreading, then twisted at the neck, a mother-of-pearl charred and melted. From the stopper rose a long, oily, needlelike filament of frozen glass that somehow never got broken. The darker streaks of color appeared translucent, and the shifting tones and light gave the impression that something moved inside, a bottle imp. The wish-granting imp was so ugly that anyone who saw it sat in shock for hours afterward. I alone could look on it without horror. "Show yourself," I said, and it lifted the teetering stopper just enough to reveal its face and one arm. Pale gray and runny with the perfume oil, it had wide nostrils into which the oil drained, eyes buried in fold upon fold of puffy flesh, the broken, flopping ears of a goat, a mouth black and wide with soft teeth that, decomposed by the oil, hung like cubes of felt. Its arm, gnarled and partly hidden under its coarse, pointed beard, ended without wrist or palm but with one thick finger.

"What do you do all day?" I asked.

"Masturbate," he said. "From that, the oil."

"I have a wish," I said. I asked to be made undivided, unlacerated, pure. He didn't respond, the stopper slithering in his grasp, the glass needle circling above him like an antenna. I had to be more specific. I explained that by pure I meant someone for whom there was no separation between her and anyone or anything.

"You are what you're made of and what you will be, dead."

"There's nothing else?"

"What is your mother now?"

~

Ben whimpered in his crate in the dark. Every time Marge moved in her bed, he earnestly thwacked his half-tail on the bars. The other dogs ignored him, understanding that he was intent on something that didn't involve them—getting back to the smells and spaces he belonged in, the angles and odors of Ritter's body, the pungency of his crotch. Marge knew Ritter's crotch, its smell of sweat and skin-packaged semen, wrapped in the loose, porous pelt and gnarly hair, although she had never even seen it. Alone in bed, Marge saw how the grain of Ritter's skin changed from his nipples to his underarms, missing only the weight of his body on her mattress. Without guilt she could explore him with her mind's eye, finger, and tongue, because after three years of friendship they had the feel of relatives, and her mind could treat him the way it did Scofield and her favorite dogs, whose every freckle she knew, the way it would have treated her children had she not, after two miscarriages and a prolapsed uterus, passed them up for a career in real estate and dogs. When he married Marge, Scofield was a member of the K-9 police force, and Marge was getting a stout insurance settlement, which she invested in real estate so that she and Scofield would have enough to start and keep their dog farm. The insurance settlement came from a riding accident on her father's land—two poachers frightened her horse, who then broke his leg in a gopher hole and fell on Marge, breaking her back.

Alone in bed in her camper, Marge wondered what proof there was that her memory was accurate. Her back hurt sometimes, but so did many backs not fallen upon by quarter horses. She knew she owned dogs, or at least that she had contact with dogs, because she heard them sleeping. There was no proof that she owned eight champions, or that K-9 City existed. She knew the day with Ritter had been real because she could hear Ben crying, taste traces of a

T-bone in her mouth, and feel the adrenaline spiral from her stomach out of tension or thrill, she couldn't tell the difference. She couldn't feel her wedding ring without moving her fingers, but even so Scofield filled the camper and breathed her breath. She had not slept with Ritter—her inner thighs did not ache, saddle-sore, and no wetness dampened her panties. Sleeping with him was possible: Scofield could die, but as it was, Scofield's prominence hung about her so closely that even Ritter didn't approach her. He let himself love her, knowing Scofield invisibly guarded her body, sweat through her skin, interrupted her mind's voice. In her half-sleep, Scofield's weight tilted the camper on its shocks. He cuffed the dogs and they swarmed; he blew the camper's horn and shoved her onto her stomach. Alarmingly naked, she waited, knowing her body, plump in clothes, had the power of voluptuousness when undressed. Scofield loved to undo her in the night. He often woke her up before dawn by mounting her from behind. She preferred it, because it asked only that she rock her hips backward, let him bite her neck, and otherwise stay asleep. She rarely remembered anything on waking in the morning, only knowing what had happened when she stood up. He needed her. Neither would betray the other; K-9 City could never survive a divorce.

~

"Bring your shoulder bag," Scofield says to Officer Phelan. "My niece is going to walk up just before the decoy comes to try to take the bag. Walk around a few times, then sit by the board. Put the bag in front of George."

Phelan's German shepherd George is rigged with a harness and leash for control and a choke chain and leash for correction. He heels obediently, with a nonchalant awareness of the dangerous weapon that he is. Like all good police dogs, he is healthy, powerful, and exceedingly confident. He obeys only Phelan, and obeys him almost completely. Two years ago George was froggy, jumping and snarling at anything that moved. Scofield taught Phelan how to fix that without beating the dog lifeless. A froggy animal needs to channel his fear and aggression into confidence, obedience, and discernment. To gain confidence, the dog should play tug-of-war with family members and be allowed to win. He should think he's next in line for the alpha male position, which the officer holds. With his pack position secure, he'll be less vicious. For obedience, the officer should severely punish the dog's every act of irrational and unprovoked wickedness by hanging him by the scruff, shaking him, and swinging him around, which doesn't hurt so much as it humiliates, with the added benefit of making the dog helpless. Once George growled when Phelan approached his rawhide chew, and Phelan hung him like that for five minutes. He said his arm muscles hurt for days afterward, but it was worth it. George is still wild; Scofield can see it in the way he prances and whirls around before sitting. The difference is, now George thinks before angering Phelan. It makes Scofield proud to see him working, all dynamic alertness *and* potent compliance. Phelan heads George toward the board, a small wooden wall cemented into the ground, to which less experienced dogs are bolted during agitation exercises. Phelan puts the bag in front of him, and George licks his teeth tensely. He knows this place is where men-vermin harass him, provoke him to the point of a brawl that he always wins.

A few dozen yards away, Cam approaches on schedule. "Tell your dog *at ease,* then let him relax, paw around a bit. You sit on the ground and without giving anything away, brace yourself," Scofield says. He and Phelan watch Cam and watch the dog, whose attention is on the girl. The dog stands up, front paws on each side of the bag. He whines and looks to Phelan, confused, and then again watches Cam, who, with her short brown curls bouncing and shining in the low autumn sun, smiles at Phelan.

"Just walk by," Scofield says. "Stop at that tree and wait there." George growls to himself as Cam passes, but has learned that he is not to attack any stranger who does not suspiciously hide things in his clothes, then face him with a weapon. Scofield, for a split second, half wishes to see Cam toppling under George's leap, to hear the bones of her unprotected forearm snap in his blood-splashed mouth. Scofield can make it happen.

Over the last few months he has grown convinced that there is something just plain unnatural about this braless girl. She never speaks about what she does in school or after school. When a teenager calls for her, the discussion centers around history or band practice and ends abruptly. But her coldness is not what frightens him; it's something deeper. She is about as involved in his daily life as a cloud; lofty, unreachable, superior, indifferent, she floats above him, chilling him, oppressing him. His fantasies of mastery and rape, he decides, are a normal intellectual reaction to her frustrating personality. She launches his imagination into a flight of compensation, forcing him to fill in what is behind her innocent front—a skewed demonic ghost conjuror with the most vibrant stretch of young flesh imaginable. Sometimes she sits right beside him on the couch, unreachable, and yet it would be so easy to flip her over and pierce her concealed cryptic brown eye, invade her hidden catacombs of filth. He can end his torture by killing the source. An accident with a dog like George would do it.

The decoy—in this case, an officer from another district who volunteers to get himself attacked—strolls along the same path Cam took, hiding behind him one arm wrapped in heavy inner-tube rubber and a burlap sack, a gauntlet, and a gun. When he is just a few feet away, George barks, and the decoy turns on him, aiming the gun at his head, snatching for the bag at his paws. In a flourish of muscle-driven bone pistons, George pitches into the man and clamps his jaws into the burlap. With his other hand and a switch, the decoy stings the dog's flanks, but the pain goads George into tugging with backward thrusts of his hind legs, and Phelan stands behind him, hanging on the leashes and shouting to Scofield, and the decoy falls forward on his knees, then sprawls onto his stomach, and George is a doll-eyed shark, a horn-scissoring bull, and Phelan yells, and Scofield waves for him to pipe down, he'll call the dog off in a minute, and he waits until he hears Cam's thin voice: "What's going on?"

~

When I realized I hadn't bled for about six weeks, I was in my room, neither reading nor playing my flute. Tim quit his job at K-9 City, so I had to call him up to tell him about my missed period. I sat by my window and watched the dogs pant in the shadows of their pens. The last time I had my period was on a bright muggy day when somebody didn't do somebody else's job, and Aunt Marge and I ended up hosing down the kennels ourselves. The runs had to be washed daily, especially in the summer, to keep down the worms and parasites, flies and maggots. Mosquitoes spawned their larvae in the dogs' water buckets. Inside the narrow, rank kennel hallway, I banged on the chain-link until each dog rocketed into its pen, its nose and lips bunched on its muzzle, roaring like a garbage disposal. I released the hook and string that dropped a guillotine door behind the dog, and that way the run was safe for Aunt Marge to clean.

In the puppy kennels, the young littermates were the most difficult. Packed together by fours and fives, they didn't fit into the inner pen, and I had to put them all on leads so that they scratched me up with their claws and puppy teeth instead of leaping on Aunt Marge, who was busy. She took the young bloodhounds, nine months old, unsold, untrained, ignored, destined to become so untractable as to live out their lives at K-9 City in the narrow run. I saw how strong Aunt Marge was; her forearms rippled under thin, freckled skin. The pups' fur stuck to my wet and sweaty arms and legs, and I imagined, with the cramps swelling, my stomach fluttering nauseous, and my head buzzing, that I was one of the dogs. I held the German shepherds' leads and crouched down among them, and they put their open mouths, bloody with loose puppy teeth, on each other and on me equally. Looking over each other's backs, we were excited that Aunt Marge had come to clean, not because the abundance of droppings and urine offended our sensitive noses, but because she was Aunt Marge and she was near us, scraping and hosing and moving.

The pups all seemed to like each other.

I wasn't sure if my last period had begun that day, six weeks before. I didn't ask Aunt Marge how much time had passed since she and I cleaned the kennels because it would have been none of her business why I was asking. I figured I was probably pregnant, and my baby, which I meant to keep this time, would be Aunt Marge's business soon enough.

Looking out my bedroom window, I could see over the treetops and thought that somewhere in space and time was my old hometown and my old house and the old medical center, where just under a year before, Dr. Harris asked me to fetch my parents from the waiting room. I brought him Mr. Dheil, who introduced himself as my grandfather. Dr. Harris gave him a speech about how appalling it was that so many very young girls were sexually active. He didn't want to shock Mr. Dheil, but this little girl had had frequent vaginal and anal intercourse. Mr. Dheil shouted at me, then, with his hands doing a remarkable imitation of quivering arthritis, stroked my hair. Either I was abused by someone in the family, Dr. Harris went on, or I had done some wayward experimentation with an older schoolboy. He asked if I had been away at camp. I finally lied that there was, in fact, an older boyfriend who said sex was safe until I had my first period, and couldn't help searching Mr. Dheil's face for some sign that he felt foolish. Dr. Harris, with his righteously white hair, stood under the photograph of the plane he always wanted and now owned and said that I was an irresponsible, selfish girl who gave no thought to the shame I brought to my relatives. He suggested that both families have a long talk, because I was pregnant, well into my second trimester. Pregnancy at my age was a serious health threat. He recommended immediate termination.

Driving home in the car, Mr. Dheil argued with me like a boyfriend. From the way he explained why we shouldn't get married, I saw that he had considered it, recognizing me, in some sense, as an equal, which even I could tell was ridiculous. My power to incubate life frightened him, and so did his own power to extinguish it with reason and intimidation. Life-incubation was not really a power—I was nothing more than a commissioned barge carrying a stranger from shore to shore. To wish to keep the baby was to indulge my own adolescent maternal instincts, ignorant, whimsical, shortsighted— this was the gist of, the truth in, Mr. Dheil's rationalizations. Defining myself as a mother was aggrandizing a simple biological accident that could easily be corrected.

I imagined Mr. Dheil would marry me, since, from what Grandmom Modery had taught me, abortion was unthinkable. Plenty of Aborigine girls had babies at my age. If Mr. Dheil and I married, our love would finally be public, and I could live with him in his pretty colonial house with its great white rooms, and his friends could still come and take me; I could live this way a long time. I saw myself walking, with an adult smile, out of the afternoon bedroom to check on my child. "Excuse me," I said to the man in the bed. "I think I hear my baby."

A dandelion-haired girl stood in a crib.

I imagined I sat in the bathroom pressing wads of toilet paper between my legs, the way I always did. From there I often heard the men talking downstairs, but this time I heard one offer a lot of money for sex with my little girl.

I put clothes on and took the baby out the back door. The snow crunching thick on the ground and the wind shimmering with snow powder, I walked into the middle of a field, even though there was no field behind Mr. Dheil's house. After undressing the baby in the dry cold, I laid her in the snow, where she fit like precious merchandise in Styrofoam. Her skin turned thick white and her face frowned hard, but she made no sound as I walked to the house.

"I had Harris make an appointment for you out-of-state," Mr.

Dheil said in the car on the way home. "And I've got a friend in Bricktown who can get you a diaphragm. It's not your fault."

For the first time I put my hands on my stomach in that way, because I realized she wasn't in the doctor's words or in my mind or frozen in snow, but in the car with us, under my blouse, my swollen belly, my fingers, alive.

In my bedroom, I left the window overlooking the rows of K-9 City kennels, and I lay down on my bed and put my face in the pillow. I had a strong desire to go swimming in a dark room. Mr. Dheil's baby had been a wonder, a mystery, stolen from me by all the busy fathers that ever hurried in the world; she escaped—now she lived, I believed, somewhere under the treetops, someone's adopted daughter. I lay on my stomach, and between my spine and the mattress pressed a new baby, an invasion, a parasite, feeding and breathing from my blood, growing, and crowding my organs.

～

Scofield, going down the cellar stairs with a sack of dog chow, notices a spot on the wall near a step. He sets the sack down and touches it with his fingers. It feels more like a dent than a smudge. On his way back up he brings a flashlight, to get a good look. It turns out to be neither a smudge nor a dent, but a burn in the shape of a paw print. The scuffed and cracked steps show no such marks. It's a large print, maybe four, four and a half inches across. He tries to imagine how a dog could turn its leg like that to make the print; then he realizes that it must have been made as the house was being built sometime in the late 1800s. A dog must have trotted through some corrosive chemical, then stepped on the wall-board as he yelped and bounced. Scofield scratches at the spot with his fingernail—perhaps the paw print was originally muddy, and the dampness and bacteria rotted the wood. The mark might be that of a deformed child's hand, or just a scrape made by the heel of a boot, coincidentally appearing as a paw print.

Scofield shows it to Marge. She's in a good mood, willing to leave Deputy alone in a long *down-stay* just to humor Scofield.

"So what's the worry?" she says. "It could have been here eighty years."

Scofield is getting worried. He wants to know how come neither of them ever saw it before. How come it's so perfect, and against the

wall like that as though the dog defied either gravity or the geometry
of bone structure? He wants to know how a burn gets made this way,
this shape. He points out to her the singe and smoke above the mark.
"Only heat does that," he says.

"This is farmland," Marge says. "It might have been a child
playing with a brand."

He asks her, jokingly, if she thinks it might be a poltergeist. She
sits down at the top of the stairs, and, looking down at him, tells him
she's never heard of pyromaniacal canine poltergeists. She figures
Cam did it with a match—her adolescent idea of art.

When Cam comes home from school, he asks her about it. She says
she saw it there her first day with them and didn't think anything of
it. She says it could be a psychic message, and he'd better not paint
over it. While making dinner, Marge says that she's sure that Cam
burned the wall. Although Cam does well in school, she's emotionally
immature, almost toddlerlike, and Marge can tell that one day the girl
is going to interfere with their lives significantly. Marge pours
walnuts in a grinder, turns the handle, and says that at the first sign
of trouble they'll put her on a plane for Chicago and her father can
put up with her.

Scofield goes into his office, shuts the door, and sits down at his
desk, where he still has the day's training reports to finish. He
wonders what kind of trouble a girl like Cam could really get into—
stealing a clarinet, running away, getting herself raped. To think that
Cam could get sent away annoys him, and he would sooner bury
Marge alive, turn all his animals loose, and pay a hit man to pick off
her father than let her go. He knows the reaction is unreasonable,
extreme, and his life would certainly be more placid without her.
She'll leave in a few years anyway, off to college, marriage, or prison.
He could chain her in the attic, stuff her in a dog suit and lock her in
a kennel, or maybe just have a doll made to look like her, one of
those anatomical dolls, better than the cheap one a cop brought into
the office one day, with a shiny tuft of Barbie hair on top and a
tubular O for a mouth. And it wouldn't be life-sized. It would only be
as big as a possum, or maybe a squirrel, and would quiver with
battery-operated shudders and make no sound.

∼

In the town library, in the hazy sunlight piddling through a dirty
window, I read that my mother's perfume, patchouli essential oil,
extracted from the East Indian shrubbery mort, is used in perfume

formulations to give a long-lasting Oriental aroma to soaps and cosmetics. Since it was also used in dyes, the authenticity of Indian shawls could be identified by the odor of patchouli, but with the wide use of the scent the test became worthless.

Yellowish to greenish brown liquid with the pleasant fragrance of summer flowers, patchouli may produce an allergic reaction in hypersensitive individuals. It has, in concentrate, the uncanny stink of goat. The cause of its distinctive aroma is unknown. The oil contains a solid body, patchouli camphor, which has little or no odoriferous value. The sesquiterpene occurring naturally in the oil is a cadinene, but as this body occurs in juniper oil and in oil of cade, the odorous substance of patchouli oil is still a mystery.

In a book with a chapter on the Hindu use of perfume oils, I came across funeral applications. Before death, the book said, passages concerning paradisal happiness are read to the dying, and a few drops of honey are placed in the mouth to satisfy agony and to counteract the temptation to take the sweetmeats offered by the evil one who lies in wait.

After death, the eyes and mouth are closed. The body is laid out for viewing and garlanded, with a lamp placed at the head to light the way to the afterlife. The nostrils are plugged with batts, the big toes tied together, the hands positioned across the chest, and the navel smeared with sexually redolent patchouli. For communities where burial is in the squatting posture, corresponding adjustments are made before the onset of rigor mortis.

For the funeral, the head is anointed with patchouli oil, soap-nut powder, and other preparations. Friends and relatives herd around the body to establish, for anyone who cares to find out, that the death was natural and was not suicide, murder, or any other violent end. Because close contact with the dead is defiling, the people hire specialists to perform further necessary intimacies.

Before cremation, the body is immersed in the holy waters of a river, then smeared liberally with clarified butter, or ghi, and laid on a pyre. The chief mourner, usually a son, lights it. Those who have come to honor the dead march around the pyre, forbidden to gaze into the flames. They are expected, however, to see to it that the skull bursts in the burning. At death the soul is trapped in the skull and must be released. Since the skull does not always explode, and since, when it does, it splatters the circling grievers, often it is first broken by blows with a cudgel.

They pray, *All that is low must perish, all that is high must fall, all complex bodies must be dissolved, and all life must terminate in* *death. When a five-element body reverts to its five components, what* *room is there for sorrow?* What room?

≈

With Marge away for the weekend he's not sure where, Scofield has time to loll around by himself. Except for a Saturday morning class with novices, he has little to do. He finds himself going over old notes in front of the television Friday night, while Cam, as always, has shut herself in her room with her books, detective magazines, sheet music, clothes: a smelly rubble in which she probably studies, dozes, writes letters—although he has never seen her receive one, mail one, or ask for a stamp—and masturbates. Scofield flips through the pay TV channels with the remote control, looking for something racy. Nearly two years have passed since he promised Marge he would stop renting the porn films he had wallowed in since the early days of their marriage. She argued that the films corrupted them both with a kind of emotional stagnation, that the variety deceived—in the end, no matter how many different teddies ripped in different sets of bad teeth in varied yet readily recognizable settings and situations, the intention and the effect were the same every time. Frankly, porn bored her and bogged her down.

He pauses for a few minutes and watches some Friday night drama series, the kind that devotes fragments of time—three minutes, seven minutes—to following the frayed, convoluted plot lines of several individual characters, only occasionally dropping a reference to time or place—a plot utensil—loudly on the enamel of illusion.

As he did back in the first post-porn days, he prefers his imagination to television, especially in his randy moments, and he remembers how he fantasized about the fate of Wild Julia. For himself, in those days, he wove a story that far surpassed any of the porn films, a story intended not only to goad his loins into cramped salivation, but to seize his very soul and slam it against the mirror of truth, in which his soul saw and lived its essence, a brawling, murderous necrophile, exciting in it a celebration of its unlimited powers of lust and a scalding self-recognition, ripping off its mask and exposing the wormlike white nerve endings of its own fearsome, loathsome self-annihilation. He tries again to imagine the story afresh, but finds instead that he is able to remember only what he already imagined, distant, stale, dead. He tells himself again the story—sees it as though on a screen—of Wild Julia, a girl already defiled and fallen, stolen away to a distant cabin, where several men—some of them vaguely but thrillingly familiar to Scofield—chased her and belted her about, ripped her clothes, and during indistinct and uncountable rapes focused the camera on her swollen and distraught face as they beat it, and on her vagina as they opened and prodded it with the muzzles of their rifles, and plunged their cocks into wounds sliced in the bruised and bloodied flesh of Julia's plump upper arms, breasts, and buttocks to the sound of her dry and near-voiceless screams.

Then, in what seems to be the climax of the film, for Scofield one of the most faintingly sublime moments, two men held her down on a cot while a third screwed her and strangled her as he came. Scofield contemplates the stunning poetry of his private, insubstantial creation, the man's sex sweat splashed into her death sweat, his thrusts choreographed to her convulsions, his life-giving sperm spawned into the fresh death-collapse of her body's hollows. Scofield surprises himself again by feeling no tremor of nausea as he watches in his mind's eye the naked, blood-lathered men noisily dismember the body and masturbate with the large pieces, spewing onto the newly butchered meat the pink sauce of their glands. Even though the story plays in his memory instead of in his more vivid imagination, it has the same revitalizing effect. His mind pulses second-to-second, disjointed by the supreme naughtiness of the ideas he has patronized. In his pants, his unrelieved penis stands erect, an untouched gauge to his unbeatable high. A strange brand of self-created vicariousness, this story of men raping and mutilating a local victim was for Scofield his rite of passage, in absentia. The only orgasm worthy of the rediscovery of his old mental snuff flick is a deep bath into which he plans to topple his body, now crippled by the cancerous swell in his pants, to set his mind to remembering the sweet, unspoiled, soapy little girl.

He puts aside his notes, turns off the TV, and heads toward the stairs, only to recall the ghost dog—Barghest, as he now calls it. He hasn't seen it for about a month, and yet it continues to have its own life somehow outside his mind, a vision produced by his conscience, his madness, yet untractable, undisciplined by his mental police. Like the hounds in dreams, it appears at its own will, incongruous with its surroundings or the rising action, neither supplementing nor contrasting the trajectory of his passions. It neither offends nor attacks him; it possesses all the box-built, heavy-headed amiability of real-life Newfoundlands. He can't walk up or down the stairs anymore without the thought of Barghest depressing him.

~

Father Robert sat on the glassed-in back porch on a squeaky wicker chair, waiting for Cam's mother to make him a cup of dong quai tea. Cam was asleep on the living room rug, surrounded by about fifty tiny ceramic animal figurines. Through open windows, summerlike breezes drifted in, carrying the distant drones of a lawnmower and a power saw, and the oniony smell of cut grass. The little girl's sleep made the whole world somnolent, he thought. His interest in her began and remained, he knew, because her ladylike frame and the mousy opulence of her hair made her a perfect Caucasian specimen. He knew such attitudes weren't befitting a priest; they smacked of supremacy, but he didn't indulge them seriously—they were harmless, like following the career of a well-gaited racehorse. All souls might have been created equal, but the fact remained that there was no democracy of flesh. Once her grandmother assured him that Cam had not been and would not be abused, that she was just a "sourpuss," his consternation became fascination, and hearing about Cam became a kind of hobby of his. Her mother, barefoot in an off-white robe, brought him a mug of tea, already steeped and sweetened. The mug looked handmade, and the handle had been broken and glued back together. "It smells like food," he said. "Like curry?" He tried not to appear as if open-mindedness were an effort.

"Ginger," she said, resting her mug deeply in her lap. The handle of her mug was intact.

He lifted the tea to his lips, but she told him it would scald his tongue. "Just wait," she said, and he was suddenly impatient. They had nothing to talk about. He stopped by only because Cam's grandmother Anne had offered to take him to lunch and said she would meet him there. This woman had met him at the door instead, and said lunch was canceled; Anne got called away by the country club for which she organized golf tournaments. Now here he sat on a back porch with someone who appeared to be smiling placidly at a tree.

"What's in the tea?" he said loudly.

"That cardinal looks as if he's watching us; it's weird," she said. The tree held a fat scarlet bird, which frisked back and forth on his branch, cocking his head intently their way. "The tea's made of licorice, ginger, cloves, dong quai, fo ti, yams, and cinnamon bark," she said slowly, as though naming each item as it passed her on a conveyor belt.

She sipped her tea, so Father Robert tried it. Indeed, it was a mouthful of liquid food, which, once swallowed, smeared a strange, sweet aftertaste up the back of his palate well into his sinuses. He thought carefully about what had just happened in his nasal cavities, and decided he didn't like it—or the pale mother of his nonpareil. Maybe she just wasn't good at conversation; maybe she was as shy and uncomfortable as he. Maybe she was offering some kind of Eastern hospitality to match her tea, an opportunity to relax, think, pray without the distraction of aloneness.

"So," he said, the practiced diplomat, the febrifuger of thousands of overheated moments. "What is dong quai?"

"Woman root. A long, yellow, fleshy root," she said. Her straight blond hair tickled in and out of the open front of her robe, and he wondered how she could stand it. "You know—like ginseng is man root."

Just when he began to ask about Cam, she thudded drearily onto the porch, buried her sleepy head in her mother's chest, and threw one leg over her lap.

"Did you pick up your porcelain zoo?" her mother said, and Cam didn't reply. "Why don't you get Father something else to drink? He doesn't like woman root."

Cam jerked her head to face him, wide awake. The size of her eyes startled him. She wrinkled her nose. "I don't blame you," she said with conspiracy. "I hate it."

The cardinal bluntly struck the window. Cam ran to the glass. "He's on the ground."

"I have to tape newspaper over the glass every spring," Cam's mother said. She wore her empty tea mug like a ring, a great clay gem against the back of her hand.

Father Robert suggested he leave.

"Every spring," Cam's mother said, "or that bird won't get anything done."

"He's still on the ground," Cam said, her forehead pressed against the glass.

Father Robert stood up, and so did Cam's mother. They moved into the kitchen, where expensive green-and-white checkered curtains tried to muffle the breezes. Glass shelves ribbed the windows, supporting rows of small herblike plants and seedlings. Some kind of ivy swung heavily from a hook, and its branches clawed their way across the ceiling and down the one indoor brick wall. On the brick hung antique iron and copper cookware, but it did not look colonial American. Off to one side hung something like a huge hammer on a broom handle.

"A poleax," Cam's mother said, "used to kill animals like cows."

The squat breakfast table and chairs, roughly hacked out of some near-black wood, their joints braced by unfinished copper clasps, looked too heavy to move. Tiny seed hulls littered the lacy green cloth that covered the table; hanging in a cage on the wall nearby sat a silent, lone cockatiel.

"My father raised pigeons," Father Robert said. The cabinet doors boasted ornate brass handles rather than knobs, glass jars full of variously colored beans, powders, and pastas lined the counter, a yellow blanket heaped itself on the floor by the refrigerator, and an open, store-bought box of dong quai tea sat near the stove.

"The red bird flew away," Cam said, and walked across the kitchen, waded through the yellow blanket, and, reaching up, hauled open the refrigerator door. "Well," she said. "What would you like?"

~

Marge and Ritter knew each other now the way spouses and lovers do. After meeting again at a dog show in Pittsburgh, they joined several others for a party in a hotel room, then went out dancing. Marge always disdained people who used dogs and dog shows as an excuse for behaving like college kids on a Florida spring break, abandoning their dogs to thirst and fear in strange dark rooms, making more noise in the wee hours than a pack of wailing bloodhound pups, throwing up on hotel carpets, pissing into hotel sinks, and passing out to leave the feeding and walking of their dogs either to their more sober companions or to no one. Tired of Scofield's burdensome moods, she let Ritter lead her off with his friends and joined the crowds of irresponsible yet happy dog owners. Although a little drunk and realizing she could be the mother of almost everyone in the nightclub, Marge danced with Ritter several times, quickly relaxed, and picked up the words and rhythms of songs that usually annoyed her. The shape of Ritter's back excited her, a neat trapezoid, the long line of his shoulders parallel to the short line of his belt. He moved with choppy nonchalance, which she complemented with smooth undulations of her hips, dipping her shoulders coyly and absorbing herself in her own body's grace. When they left the club, she was sweaty, breathless, and not at all drunk. She said goodnight to him with a long, simple hug at her camper door.

As the dogs shuffled impatiently in their crates, Ritter's body was unfamiliar yet without surprise in the trickle of gray sunrise around the blinds of the camper windows. He knocked on her door at five a.m. and caught her the way Scofield often did, awash in immobilizing sleep juices, unable to wake fully amid her warm body odors, defenseless in the gullet of dawn.

She let him in dreamily and drew him to the bed. She saw that his skin was so hairless and taut across his sinews as to appear invisible. Her tongue could almost lift a muscle segment from the bone like the meat of a well-cooked chicken wing. He hummed to her, his leanness arched above, moving to his music. He made of them two ballet dancers, two moving images in a sculptor's eye, at once music upon motion and form upon porcelain. Standing, balancing beside the bed, they struck poses of picturesque connection, both creating with the same harmonics in mind, the same eye for symmetry. He gave little attention to the usual linear time sport, a frustratingly tenuous balance of delay and advance toward a goal more efficiently achieved alone by hand. His only aim was that of a thespian, a landscapist, a pointillist; physical pleasure merely set different moods, chords, color schemes. Sex was all forms of art. It was the creative act and the finished product simultaneously. The father of two families the size of volleyball teams, he afterward admitted, with regret, that her hysterectomy reduced the significance.

Then Saturday's competitions passed rapidly like no others, with the memory of a not-so-strange man beside her in Scofield's traveling bed, this new man's seepage between her legs, smelling unfortunately no different from Scofield's. All day, among so many dog lovers, dog professionals, and AKC animals, she was unhappy, conscious of a loss. The loss certainly was not a schoolgirl's, nor was it at all the fear of losing her husband, home, and business. In fact, she had gained many things: an exploration of the freedoms afforded by a hysterectomy, a sexual experience, an extra dimension to her relationship with Ritter, an artistic interdependence since each was now the other's clay, and a teaspoon of semen. Yet she had lost her old self. She had reaffirmed that no matter how time seems to stand still, it in fact does not, and all the while you're busy transcending it with Danielle Steele, work, Molly Dodd, children, beer, and prayer, time is trundling on, altering everything. Decisions were never not final. If you bought an outdoor grill from Sears, then returned it, the fact remained that for a few days you owned an outdoor grill. While to be friends with Ritter in the first place was an irrevocable decision, the old friendship was irretrievable. She was now different. She was a liar.

On the way home Saturday afternoon, she wielded the camper into the parking lot of a pharmacy outside Pittsburgh, where she bought a disposable douche, used it in her camper latrine, threw it out in the pharmacy's trash bin, and was on her way again, wondering on the one hand if deception wasn't too easy, too natural, beneath her, or if it came easily because in the back of her mind she had been planning it all along, keeping secret from herself the amassed skills necessary to an accomplished lifestyle of dishonesty and freedom. As she recovered from her surgery six years before and suffered the early onslaught of menopause, had she done it all willingly not because Scofield was insistent about wanting it, but because she knew she was paying for more than his pleasure alone? Had she given up her womanhood, her bloody bond with the undeniable tides of hormones, to become a walking convenience store? In a sense, her vagina had no more function than a golf ball cleaner.

~

"Be a good little niece and take your bath." One penis is not enough; Scofield has seven. Adroitly he finds homes for them all in the crevices and cushions of the toddler's body. He wiggles and wriggles, striving for a simultaneous orgasm. The TV is on downstairs loud enough for him to hear Jane Pauley announce that all progress has come to a halt. One man finally realized what mankind really aimed for, as it conceived faster planes, deeper mines, more quickly erected high rises, microwave ovens, robots, and computers. All along, from the Roman aqueduct to fusion reactors, man has really been searching for the instant orgasm. Instead of channeling his energy into designing a smaller microchip or giving prefrontal ablations to diabetic cats, this man invented a lightweight, removable bionic device that, when worn over the penis and activated, gently and instantly induced orgasm, without the mess. There is, Jane Pauley sums up, no longer any reason for progress.

But Scofield's mistaken. He has only one penis and it's limp, and the little girl, crying, is climbing out the window. Alarmed, he grabs her before she topples two stories into the forsythia, and she turns on him and hisses, "You said you'd get me off." She slaps his tired slug, "With what?"

He pumps it with all the speed his arm can manage. He wants one of those devices, but he missed the mentioning of where and when they'd be marketed. Besides, one of those wouldn't help him satisfy this demanding child with her eyes fixed longingly on the curtain rod. He works harder on himself, but his distractions keep him soft. He tells her about a pill he heard about for women, one that induces acute masturbation, doing away with any need for a penis. She sits naked on the radiator sobbing, but then the radiator starts to steam and gyrate. She rocks herself blissfully on the pipes while her clean, virgin grease coats the metal.

"Wait!" he says. "You make no sense."

∽

I tried to talk to Mr. Dombrowski in the band room as practice broke up. So he could hear me better, he took me into his office, a narrow closet of a room, stacked with folders of paper, instrument cases, and broken, teetering music stands. He sat me in his swivel chair and cleared himself a place to sit on his desk.

"I'm not happy," I said when he seemed ready to listen. I couldn't look up; I wasn't sure why I wanted to talk to him. I knew I could very easily make a fool of myself. "I don't like music anymore."

Sitting on his desk, he smiled down at me and gave me a brief speech about the ups and downs of talented young musicians. Outside his door the band dispersed, blaring discordant, disjunctive notes and riffs as the students took apart their instruments and, shouting, talking, laughing, wandered away.

I tried to explain that my problem wouldn't, couldn't just pass; it was built into all music, which started and was over. I saw through it: music was really just an arrangement of sounds in the same way that a painting was just a rectangle of dried paint. My tongue grew thick and clumsy as I spoke, some slight fear revved in my chest, and I stopped talking, trying not to gasp audibly. I couldn't tell him that thinking I might be pregnant again had left me bound to bodies, to practicality, so resolutely that I couldn't escape anymore. If I had a baby I'd never reach my mother, never hear her say, "Cammie's all I want," instead of "One, and one's too many," the way she did when asked how many children she had.

"How are things at home?" he said.

Now I hated reading too, I told him; fleshless unions were all lies. If I didn't have my music or my books anymore, I had nothing to do at home. Ben and Darcy had to be in those kennels like the other dogs for such long spells they got funny around the eyes, they didn't trust you. I told him—just between him and me—about the white linguinis snaking in the dogs' droppings. The dogs at K-9 City had worms, and I didn't know how Uncle Scofield got away with it. Just for a second, I imagined I could go home with Mr. Dombrowski to live with him and his wife and their three green-eyed children where the music would be so constant as to absorb the very time tracks it rattled on and I could be happy.

He assured me my musical disappointments would pass, and he asked if I had a record player. I realized then that in the Scofield home there were no phonographs, no tape decks, no radios; I produced all the music. He shuffled several long minutes through a filing cabinet. Outside the door, the only sound was that of a lone tuba player practicing a part, which, isolated, sounded so strange to me I couldn't recognize what piece it was from. I wished all concert pieces were strung out, each musician playing her separate part. Albinoni's Adagio for strings would last a business week and then some. Mr. Dombrowski handed me the score to Messiaen's *Quatuor pour la fin du temps* and told me I should study the biographies of the great modern composers.

In my room that afternoon, I struggled through the violin part on my flute. Unable to transpose, I found the music awkward, but I played "Louange a' l'eternité de Jesus" several times. I felt a kinship to Messiaen's attempt at timelessness, but the relation was parallel, not connective. And, ultimately, the eternal quality of the quartet was an illusion, a trick of musical magic—circling repetitions, limited transpositions, extremely slow tempos, and metaphor. Cross-legged on the tilted bedroom floor, with Messiaen's sheet music before me and my flute, warm and greased with my fingerprints, on my lap, I was alone. I stood up and twirled my flute like a baton, smacking the keys, tossing it in the air and missing it, crashing it to the floor, a solid silver, open-holed Gemeinhardt, a half-present from the old man who said he'd write me and visit me, who actually wrote rarely and only of rose bushes and weather and visited me not once.

I wrote to him secretly and bled through my pen *there's a hotel outside town* black blood on white spiral-bound notebook paper *I used to sneak out with Timmy we spent a whole night in a tent in the woods no one knew no one watches me* blue blood on light beige Citadel music paper *visit me and we'll do like we did when we sent away the baby one year old now do you know where it is?* red blood in the staffs for erotic effect *we'll turn on the air conditioner with one sheet over we'll doze and I'll do* followed by a few hand-notated stanzas of "Flight of the Bumble Bee," to which he responded that he had a bit of trouble with his lungs and might have to have one out, had the autumn weather there been as changeable as here? the woman next door did his raking, he thought he saw my father in Woolworth's, the thing that I asked for had been incinerated, for some reason my old junior high school band would not march in the Thanksgiving Day parade this year.

~

Cam sleeps in such odd places at odd hours that Scofield can't just drop off to sleep at night anymore, afraid that she's scuffing around in the dark with her purple-circled eyes and thirsty look. "That girl is scary," he says when he hears the bathroom light click on or off, he can't tell. He can't sleep if he thinks she's awake because he's afraid she'll kill him. He tries to relax by crossing his arms over his throat, a protection against hyenas, rabid wildcats, and bats. He feels safer under the weight of his own arms, and a toddler lifts the covers at the foot of the bed and crawls up between his legs, and a big cool hand closes around his cock.

"You're hard," Marge says.

"I was falling asleep." He rolls onto his side, pulling himself out of Marge's fist.

Marge says she has to talk to him about sex. She's been masturbating lately, not too often, just a couple of times, but she needs some romance, some gratification, and that's about all Scofield hears before drifting down into sleep again, and Marge is shoving him with her hands and feet, maybe trying to roll him off the bed.

"Suppose I wanted you now, when you're out cold and can't fight me, suppose I take you?" she says. The bed shakes as though Marge is undressing. Before he can sit up she's on him, straddling him and pinning him down with her forearm across his neck.

Wide awake, he starts to laugh. "Okay, I get it," he says, and he tries to tilt her off him, but she sits on him fast. She rocks herself against him, leaving cold, wet smears on his soft cock. This isn't my wife, he thinks; this is some joke of a harlot from a magazine, some feminist she-bitch. She must have gotten an earful from a girlfriend on her last trip, and now she's trying out the advice—be aggressive, turn the tables, and you'll please him like nothing will—and Scofield is angry, wondering how she ever thought he'd fall for this pop culture shit, this role-playing revive your fucking marriage hype, and he tells her if she wants gratification to go sit under the hot water faucet.

Angering him seems to encourage her, and she croons, "Hold still, here, spread your arms out like this," trying to be artsy and masterful and dominating, so Scofield tries another tactic.

He tells her it's not working, and she's making a fool of herself, not even the worst porn flick would take her with her ass like the back of a Volkswagen and her tits like two shriveled pears, and if he didn't screw her in her sleep he wouldn't get any. She gets out of bed, puts on her housecoat in the dark, and goes downstairs. He feels a bit bad lying to Marge, whose pear breasts are cute and whose water-balloon ass he loves to swash on, and who probably would make love to him anytime he wanted except he doesn't. He wants her only when she's dead asleep because when she's awake she moves too much, tries to grip him with her arms and legs, tries to lick his beard and chew on his eyebrows, and grunts, sighs, and whistles. Even at four a.m. she yawns and stretches under him, and he just wants to take her by the hair and crack her neck or shove her face into the mattress until she's asleep again, motionless, absent, vulnerable without rights, needs, fears. No one plays the game the way his older sister did. When they were high school kids, she knew the rules just as they dawned on him, and after school she laid herself out for him in her uniform and skillfully kept her mouth slack, her eyelids twitchless, her joints torpid. Once he went too far, coming on her face, and she never quite trusted him after that, couldn't keep her eyes shut, lost her patience, and started walking out in the middle of the game.

He remembers the porch of a trailer home, rippled by the little pocketknife blades of children who wanted a piece of the bloodied wood left as a woman made her way to the lawn to die of a slit throat. It happened while Scofield was still on the police force, and even though he was assigned to the case, he never saw the body or the blood, but interviewed the neighbors, who said the couple always fought like that, had sex in front of the open windows, and he saw the story in the papers month after month, summarized and added to, qualified, and reevaluated, Husband Slits Wife's Throat on Front Porch in Full View of Neighbors. He thinks he hears Marge talking in the kitchen, and figures Cam has gone down too. The two of them kneel on the floor, Cam in her nightshirt and Marge in her housecoat, with Barghest between them, thumping its silent tail. They feed it ephemeral treats of swamp fog, evergreen pollen, and the odor of toothpaste. The three of them will stuff Scofield's throat with the fur of shedding ghost dogs and sew his lips shut with thread made from the spines of gnats.

≈

With the cold swirl of diarrhea-like pain in my gut, I sat at my bedroom window. The school nurse had said the feeling in my bowels was just stress.

I looked at the windowpane and saw my own face in it, soapstone colored against the evening dark. I looked like the woman on the cover of *The Girl in a Swing*. I imagined I'd told my father about my pregnancy, and we had to go pick him up at the airport. We see him in the distance, huffing down a hall, his heavy suitcase swinging at the end of his arm. I say to Aunt Marge, "I'm going to throw up," and she tells me I'm not going anywhere. When he comes through a gate in the steady stream of strangers, I stand leaning forward, sticking out my breasts so that in Scofield's old, large sweater, my belly won't be such a shock. He hugs us and catches Aunt Marge's eye but never mine, and his words seem twisted like yarn behind the needle eye of his lips and if he opens them the words will come snaking out and fray. I keep thinking I'm going to say "Daddy," and I try to imagine how I'm going to say it but can't.

I see myself at band practice, and they all notice the gradual change. Mr. Dombrowski never says anything, so I know he must have heard about it from the counselor and the nurses. They take me out of gym and put me in health class with the seniors. Nancy, the fourth chair, keeps asking me, "Aren't you scared?" and some days I say I am because it's going to hurt, but the worst that can happen is that I die and I stand as they say it happens in the woods or some place with a blinding light coming toward me, and I have it dead in my arms and it convulses babylike and nuzzles me, my mother looks like her live self, not stretch-faced and wax-lipped as she did, "Mom," I say, "we're home." Her eyes grin and Grandmom is there, with her disappointment dripping through her permanent wave and yet not judging me; for some reason Mr. Dheil is there too, he must have died in the meantime, and there he is and everyone knows, and I'm so happy I say to him, "There's no one like you, I knew there was a way back," and he doesn't shush me. We all stand around and look at each other a very long time.

I tell Uncle Scofield I'm going to have a baby, and I plan to go live with my father in Chicago, but instead I have Mr. Dheil come get me, and he's in the delivery room, grandfather, with his long, cool fingers on my neck as I pant and push, his fist for me to grip and pull against, his face there for me to focus on, slate blue eyes, a hook nose with its ever-present droplet of moisture at the nostril rim, his broad, bony shoulders a wall, a buffer, a cave around me on all sides so that all I know is him, all I feel is him, there is no tearing flesh, no straining bones, only him and my wailing, and as the little body passes through my shredded muscle I come with long, deep shudders, looking straight into Mr. Dheil's face.

Mr. Dheil's face was wrinkled, with strong muscles at the forehead, cheeks, and lips, not just from playing wind instruments, but from reacting as he listened. He could direct an orchestra with his expressions. For a body-sharer, he lived almost exclusively in his mind instead of in his arms or legs or back, the way most body-sharers do. His mind was music, and it spread codas across his cheeks. Sometimes, when he pressed his forehead against mine, the sound, glorified, vibrated through my brain, and in those moments I was a musician. His face directed me.

I imagined we were married, with my new little girl old enough to walk alongside the shopping cart. She and I walk up and down the aisles, choosing food for the three of us—me, Linda, and Mr. Dheil. "I want these," Linda says, and she pulls a box of Fruit Loops off the lowest shelf. In the checkout line other people can hear us talking. She stands in the cart, helping me put our purchases on the belt. "What are we going to do when Daddy dies?" she says, because Mr. Dheil is old and sick, and the exhilaration in my chest is enough to fly on.

In the bedroom window, my blue-white face looked dead at me. It shimmered, as though plastic and hollow, empty of blood and babies and imagination. I moved my lips to see how it spoke to me silently. It had a presence, it was a person, but it had no life—if I were to turn off the lamp it would disappear, its seemingly material existence dependent upon the refraction of light waves. Yet it would remain there too; when I left to brush my teeth and climb into bed, it would stay invisible and staring, its lips moving without purpose, eternally, immensely without responsibility. It smiled, a lovely face, and opened its mouth; its pointed tongue quivered out and licked mine, cold and slaking as melted ice.

~

After dinner, Scofield, in his office, fills out the day's retraining report. Cam and her mumps had not joined them for dinner; in fact, he hasn't seen her much in the last few days since she fell sick. He thinks of her as she must be now, dozing through shivers and sweats, her mouth and throat one long blister, her face distorted by disease. He decides to visit her, and in her room he is repulsed. He recoils in the doorway at the stink of filthy clothes and linens, the humidity from a spitting vaporizer, and her face, swollen as though long drowned, as though pieces of it might break off and float away.

"I'm bored to death," she says without difficulty.

Encouraged, he thinks maybe he has done the right thing coming to visit her. She looks small in the graying bedclothes, and as he nears, the light on her bedstand gives her face a plump look, like a toddler's. Her dirty hair lies flat on her head, as though stroked too much. He has no place to sit. He notices for the first time that there are no pictures on the walls.

"We should get you something to look at," he says. The only thing hanging on the wall is a calendar of dogs he gets free from a dog food company.

"Get me a TV." She says Aunt Marge won't let her go downstairs to watch TV. "It's not that she's worried I'm too sick. She just doesn't want me 'camping' down there."

Her flute lies alongside her. Scofield mentions that he hasn't heard her playing lately. She looks at him as though she thinks he's the stupidest, most tiresome person she's ever seen, then shows him how she plays with just the keys. She calls it "key slapping," and a soft, popping tune comes off the flute.

To himself, he marvels. All he has tried to teach her about dog training is so little compared to what he feels he wants to teach her, and even less compared to what she knows about music. His twelve years of K-9 service will never compel her to wonder over him the way he sometimes wonders at her music, an alien world of abstraction and sound, incomparably removed from his world of dogs and bodies. The only mystery in his work that approaches her realm is scent detection—article, bomb, and narcotics tracking. For a short time he worked with cadaver detection, but the training tools were too hard to acquire. He decides he'll teach her narcotics detection as soon as she's well, wowing her with the apparatus of drugs, tubes, vials, and minuscule plastic bags of controlled substances granted to his professional use by the police department. He would rather get into cadavers again, seeing her stare at the carefully wrapped and labeled cubes of gray human meat, seeing her run along behind a gleaming ripple of Doberman muscle, the dog's mind on the game and its nose full of death.

She fixes her eyes on the blank wall, and her fingers keep up their rapid tok-tokking on the flute. He leaves her alone, and when he sees it's still early in the evening, he gets in his car and drives off to buy her a new television. He can't figure out if he's being extravagant or not, since he doesn't know how long she'll be sick or if she'll realize how generous he's being. Her illness, her sickly ugliness, has freed him, momentarily, and he can love her like an uncle, which is a sometime father. He finds himself thinking with excitement about the days when she'll be well again and he will have given her this great impetuous gift, shortly before and in spite of Christmas. He'll hear the new TV talking to itself late at night, talking to her, blinking at her blue nudity, a square, twelve-inch eye—his. In his car in the dark, every road seems to stretch and beckon across the whole continent, and he wonders about his true motives. This desire to befriend her is an ache, good and natural to him. His interest in dogs started from this same need to be peaceful, affable. As a young boy delivering papers, he ran across hostile dogs and managed to make friends with them all, and each granted him immunity. He took time to play with them, especially with the bigger, more dangerous ones, and he taught them games with old tennis balls. Yet a dog has never been more indifferent than this teenage girl, and he's not sure why he forgets about her for weeks sometimes, just stops thinking about her, stops noticing her, almost to protect himself, but perhaps to spite her, or perhaps out of tiring perplexity. Then, he may hear her tinkling on the toilet, or notice her skirt wedged in the cleavage of her buttocks, or find one of her toenail clippings on the carpet and take a few minutes to go off by himself and scratch himself with it, chew on it, and, unwilling to throw it away, swallow it.

Whether or not he's preoccupied by her, he sometimes sees the dog ghost in the house or dreams about it, and almost always confuses it with her, the way his father would sometimes call him by his sister's name and never realize the mistake. But he never mistakes Camille for anything but herself or anything he's come to learn about the name— a movie, a model, a sculptress, a novel, a stimulant, a tonic, a freedom, an emmenagogue, a perfection, an anodyne, a young ceremonial girl, a sweet orange, a Volscian queen. He hates when she bleeds like a woman; he finds her pads shocking red in the garbage, but she is a bleeder, a purger of possible pregnancies, at once fertile and invitingly barren, too impossibly young to ever pass anything but blood. He pictures himself pushing into that slurping blood and then realizes he has yet another erection. He's had more in the last few months than he ever had during puberty, and these moments are when he hates Cam. He pulls into the department store parking lot and is so fucking tired of her he feels like getting out and slamming his cock in the car door. He grinds his forehead against the steering wheel, he looks around the dashboard for something to fuck; he wants to punch himself in the groin, electrocute himself in the console, scorch his dick in the cigarette lighter. He's sweating, he's sobbing, he would fuck one of his dogs if it were with him, he'd rape any woman who walked by, he wants to know why, why this is happening to him now, why she does this to him, why didn't he want her minutes ago when he had her in her bed, when Marge was down in the kitchen with the dishwasher churning, when he could have thrown aside the lovely, pungent fabric and taken her faded skin in his paws and thrust anywhere against it, just once is all it would take, anywhere, especially that swollen face, the eyes like bruises, the lips parched and parted with infection, and he struggles out of the car as though Cam were in it grabbing for him with her face dissolving into moldy pieces.

~

Sick with mumps, I spent long days in bed, medicine and mild drinks with fancy straws on the nightstand. I learned to use my tongue to make the straw opening smaller, so that the liquid molecules slid in a narrow queue over my inflamed membranes and my throat didn't have to go through the conspicuous paroxysm of a swallow. Uncle Scofield bought a portable TV for my dresser, and Aunt Marge let Ben visit. I got my period and the mumps at the same time. Mumps attack the salivary glands, and sometimes the ovaries too, the doctor told me. The stress of the virus *Rubula inflans* had delayed menstruation until both flared at once.

I had been more alone that week than I could remember ever being, even though I thought I was two, sharing in my body the same meals, the same restlessness, the same stiff neck and jaw. I was alone because no one else knew I was two, not even the second me, and I couldn't tell anyone else because I couldn't think of a way, or a reason, to tell anyone else I had made myself a murderer. I meant to kill Tim's baby for reasons that had nothing to do with Tim. Mr. Dheil was responsible for my first baby, and in that there had been hope, room for me to love what I created. Tim's baby—mine alone—scared me. I saw for the first time how much shame was inherent in pregnancy—not in pregnancy, but in me—I was just a flap of slick skin, and when pregnant cut into a circle and laid in a petri dish for a spore to grow in and everyone to see it growing, to see I was nothing more. I stood naked on the edge of the bathtub in front of the medicine chest mirror, and I punched my hips until they were black. And then there was shame in not being pregnant when so much spore-pumping had been done and I had invited it, put my fingers in my ribs and pulled myself open wide for it, spent my life baring to the air my quivering innards and muscles and coaxing that rank foam into washing over my glossy blue and pink, and some fell on my skin where my pores devoured it up, and some dripped over my bones which gave nothing to grow in, and some shot up into my brain where it was scorched, and some streamed through my esophagus and stomach where I choked it, but some squirted into good mucus where I couldn't wither, scorch, or choke it, and there it took root and threatened to bring forth fruit, thirtyfold, sixtyfold, a hundredfold.

In some ways I was sorry to have only the mumps and not a baby, because in the last week I had given birth in every conscious moment, had miscarriages, married Mr. Dheil, Timmy, strangers, and yet my musings always returned to the probable—the "school trip" that took me secretly to Maryland, where other women gave me a very special douche of salt. And there was spite in that trip to Maryland, spite and destiny, because my child's body could have held my mother's soul. That I was only sick and not pregnant smacked of a righteous dirty trick. It made me think of Fate and of God, of an omnipresent, self-serving Designer, an Engineer drawing up blueprints to make himself smile at his own uncanniness. When I found out I had the mumps, I cried in the school nurse's office, I cried again in front of Aunt Marge's G.P. when he gave me the medicine that made illness actual, I cried during my weekly phone call to my father, telling him I was sick, and again in the darkest part of my mind, in the shower, where I turned off the lights and shut my eyes so that the walls and the shower curtain opened into space and all that existed was the sound and heat of water. When I stood without touching the walls, the dark gave me vertigo, and in the wide-open black rain I moaned, not caring who heard me; I flew straight to a dead star where madness was not startling, where the composite of my dreams and consciousness collapsed, the absurd star where there never was a God.

≈

Marge stood at the kitchen sink rinsing the dog hair off her hands and arms when Cam, nearly recovered from her mumps, came through the screen door carrying a long, thin, white, wet ribbon in her fingers. It squirmed. "What is this?" she said, holding it over the sink.

"Oh God," Marge gagged, "It's a tapeworm—outside!" Her skin flinched on her bones.

"I picked it out of Ben's doo-doo," Cam said when she came back inside, brushing off her hands, then sticking her fingers under the faucet.

"Not here! God, we eat here! The bathroom—no . . ." Marge led her to the outdoor spigot. "Are you insane?" Sometimes the girl seemed to belong in an attic. She had set fire to her negligees in the bathtub, and it took the two of them six hours to scrub the soot off the walls. When Marge had chastised her, she merely responded, "I didn't know it wouldn't ventilate," and when Marge asked her what on God's great planet she was doing, she said her nightgowns were too sexy, and Marge had to agree: from what was left of them, she could see they had been naughty little smears of lace.

"I'm not insane," Cam said, drying her hands on her jeans. "I just want to know, if tapeworms are so dangerous, why are they inside the dogs?"

Marge told her straight she was making a mistake inspecting the teeth of a gift horse; she and Scofield did the best they could, and if she didn't like it her father could make other living arrangements for her. Then Cam asked if it wasn't expensive feeding all those worms, and Marge felt near striking her smart mouth. She started to explain that it was expensive and painstaking to medicate the dogs, then thought better of it, and instead promised she would cure them.

In bed that night, Marge told Scofield about the worm. "I nearly burst into tears," she said, "but I was too angry."

"She's evil, Marge," Scofield said loudly, a pent-up proclamation. "For all we know, right now she's out there in the dark eating them." He had a boyish way of exaggerating that endeared him to her, mainly because it was something unlike her, something all his own. Otherwise they were so alike that she noticed him no more than she did the empty space in her abdomen where her uterus had been. That she and Scofield shared such nearly identical traits made her affair with Ritter sensible. She was, in many ways, single. Scofield should never find out about her liaisons, because if he did they would separate in terms of opinion and emotional reaction, two distinct and offended persons, and she would in all ways then be an adulteress. The word had an exotic, adventuresome appeal, even though it addled her throughout the daylight hours with misgiving and foreboding. It made her lose weight. She was sexier with her thinning figure and her worldly eyes, happier in an uncomfortable way, and kinder to Scofield, who remained stoically ignorant of her doings. He breathed heavy peanut steam softly into the groove of his pillow.

~

The sun hovers low behind the kennels as Scofield crosses the lawn with leashes and harnesses strung over his shoulder. The autumn leaves hiss aridly from their branches and along the ground. With Marge out of town again, he has to cook dinner for himself and Cam, and he thinks, tired and stressed from a long day, instead they'll go out for fast food now that Cam is well again. He shivers and wonders if tonight they'll have the first frost. He stops walking and tries to see the huff of his breath in the air, but can't. He notices Cam looking down at him from her bedroom window and he smiles up at her, but she continues to stare. He wonders how clearly she can see his face and thinks to wave, then shocks himself with the idea that this is a moment of magnificence, she above, silent and sheltered, he below, sweaty and accomplished, communing together through a meditative gaze. The longer their eyes lock the more promise blooms in his bitter heart, and he exalts, ignoring the damp cold in the kennels' long shadows. Suddenly she's gone. A blink is too brief for her to complete the act of stepping away from the window without him seeing her move. Perhaps he has been so transported in his thoughts as not to notice her missing several full minutes. Bathed in sideways evening sunlight, he is no longer cold. He turns; the sapling he planted is gone, and he curses his hired hands until he sees that the kennels, having disappeared as well, cast no shadow on him or the house. Dizzy, he wheels to get his bearings; obviously the girl has cast some spell, or it's fatigue, a heart attack, epilepsy.

Maybe somehow he's lost in a neighbor's yard. Schizophrenic, his other personality walked him here, then dumped him back in his body. It could be days or months later, but the leashes and harnesses slump in a tangle of nylon and leather down his arm. In the distant cover of leaves at the border of the woods, a kneeling man beats a cowering black dog with a short, thick stick. Hurrying toward him, Scofield prepares his words: "Hey buddy, there's no need for that. Say, I'm lost . . ." As he nears, he sees the dog is a Newfoundland, and things start to make sense: the dog runs off and breaks into neighbors' homes, and that's why his master's kicking the shit out of him. The man, absorbed in the rhythm and the sound of the stick, does not look up, nor does the dog, flat on its stomach with its head to one side. The man ignores Scofield, who, confused and nervous, shouts something about the legality of such a thrashing. Scofield drops the gear from his shoulder to stop the man bodily, but the man, dressed in black pants and a white dress shirt, tosses the stick into the woods before Scofield can get to him. He then drags the dog's body soundlessly over the dead leaves, through tree trunks into the thick of evening. Scofield can tell by the electrified chain-link fence arcing through the woods that he is, in fact, on his own property. The kennels, the sapling, everything but his mind stands as it should. He runs to the house, crashes through the screen door, and chugs up the stairs. He barges into Cam's bedroom and demands to know if she saw him outside.

She is sprawled on the dusty floor, red- and wet-faced. "Yes," she says, her breath uneven; "can't you knock?"

"Did you hear anything? Like banging, or chopping wood?"

"No." Her voice breaks forcefully. "I didn't hear a knock either." From the floor she reaches up and waves him away feebly with a letter, a man's handwriting. "Leave me a*lone*."

~

Father Robert stopped at the grade school one day during recess, and from outside the fence spotted Cam standing in line for a game of kickball. A small, sturdy eight-year-old with long, untamed hair, she spoke energetically with two other girls in line. The other team had to shout for her attention when her turn came. She kicked the ball gustily, made first, and tried to steal second. Tagged out with a wallop of the ball, she ran back to her team grinning. Whatever her problems had been, Father Robert saw no trace of them now.

Months afterward, at Anne Modery's Methodist funeral, he watched Cam closely. Quiet, confused, polite, as grief-free as any child, she stood next to her parents, who were so bereaved that Father Robert regretted having judged them for the strange, lukewarm distance they usually kept. He prayed for Anne's soul, remembering her last confession.

"I'm here to confess to you, a representative of the church, the Holy Trinity, and the Mother of God herself, that I can't forgive my trespassers."

Through the screen in the dark, he recognized her voice.

"It's not so much *my* trespassers as it is sinners in general. People do terrible things without second thoughts. On the news you hear it. In my own family people have done, from what I see, unspeakable, unforgivable things."

He told her that dwelling on horror spawned horror in the heart. "It's a horrible thing to withhold forgiveness."

"I do dwell on it," she said. "I dwell on it for my granddaughter's sake. I drink it up, sweat in the night about it." She told him she heard that somewhere a man sodomized his nephew and hung him in the woods. Two teenage boys on a dare killed the one boy's mother with a hammer. A runaway fourteen-year-old girl was found murdered in a city dump—she had been known for years as a prostitute called "Little Red." Anne Modery began to cry. "Evil is everywhere," she whispered. "Thick as butter." She said that even though she didn't sin herself, sin intrigued her.

"Sensationalism," he said. He explained that that kind of evil was like pornography: it seduced and corrupted. "You won't save your granddaughter by studying evil. Study God. Pray for those with blood on their hands."

As far as she was concerned, her son-in-law was related to a rapist, she said, and her own daughter was a murderess. "Talk to me when sin's come close enough to stain *you*."

"The Holy Spirit possesses you—what brought you to confession?" he said.

"I came to declare myself," she said. "I've kept a secret. I can never show mercy again; I've smelled the breath of Satan."

He suggested that she reflect on the everyday acts of charity people did around her, that she pray for the grace to be charitable herself, and that she attend Mass regularly but abstain from the Eucharist until ready to make a true confession; he withheld absolution.

Cam's Grandmother Modery lay dead in her coffin, and Father Robert watched Cam copy the actions of the other mourners. Before leaving the funeral home, she knelt in her navy blue dress, then stood up on the kneeler so she could touch the dead hand.

She said to him, "It really does feel like clay."

/t/h/r/e/e/

counting
thunder

Scofield can take or leave Dana, except that the first time they met he was distant with fear, fury, and irritation, keeping to himself that he had just seen something like the large, black end of Barghest clear the top of the stair. Dana, this older teenager, and her new sidekick, Cam, were merciless, sneering and giggling with their feather earrings tangled in their hair. He hasn't seemed to be able to gain any respect from either of them. Marge tells him a girl like Dana respects no one; dropout drug addicts don't know what respect is. But from what he knows of her, she does all right—a tuba player in the school band, a late but near graduate, a part-time clerk at a card shop. She chooses to spend all her free time with Cam. On weekends she parks her dark blue '72 Pinto in his spot in their driveway and sleeps on the floor in Cam's room. In the middle of the night he wakes up to hear them sputtering with laughter or padding barefoot on the creaking floor in their oversized T-shirts. He eats breakfast later than usual on weekends so that he hits the kitchen when they do. They sit shamelessly cross-legged on the wood chairs, dirty toes pressing thighs, damp strips of panty fabric clearly visible. Cam glares because he's intruding somehow in his own kitchen. Cam glares, but Dana knows how to flirt with him. She says she took the last cup of coffee, but hasn't sipped it yet, and he can have it if he doesn't mind cream. And sugar. And bourbon. She makes him feel good-natured. She says the bourbon coffee doesn't taste good but it's a real kick in the duff. Cam points out that Dana is lying, that whiskey would curdle the cream. With a quick glance at each other, he and Dana recognize who the real spoilsport is, and he can leave the kitchen confident that his dignity's intact: Dana likes him, or Cam wouldn't have been so sour. But as he leaves the room with his egg sandwich, he sees the two girls exchange evil, secret, satisfied grins, and he is their fool, their transparent toady, and Marge says teenage girls are nasty, catty witches. He shouldn't let them make a schoolboy out of him; that ugly, sloppy derelict Dana behaves way beneath her nineteen years.

～

When Scofield made his confession to her, Marge didn't know what to say, not because she was surprised, which she should have been and wasn't, but because it followed naturally that *she* should confess, and she couldn't. The moment was all wrong. The moment was his; he had built to it for months, lost in his soul's dark nights, and he needed to purge himself, to set his burden on someone else's back. Telling him about Ritter would interrupt and impose, not to mention change her life. To confess, and in so doing relinquish her affair, was just plain silly.

Cam was at Dana's, or so she said, for the evening, and Marge found Scofield lying face down on the couch, something she had never before seen him do. She sat on the coffee table beside him and asked what the matter was. Outside the window, the trees were barely discernible against the darkened sky. The hour reminded Marge how much she enjoyed getting up right before dawn, when the sky had the same deep blue cast to it, and she, rushing around alone in the dark house, got ready to set out with the dogs before sunup. As Scofield slobbered and spilled tears and small lusts, she held him, comforted him, and said remarkably astute and sympathetic things, surprising herself. Scofield cried hard without trying to speak for several minutes. In the dark, she could make out his head in her lap, his hair, and the back of his neck with its folds of not recently shaved skin. Ritter would admire her for her strength and compassion. In her mind, she told Ritter how Scofield broke down on the couch and sobbed over his secret, foolish lusts; how he actually thought in his alarmist way that Cam wasn't safe alone with him; how he believed he was losing his mind. She would tell Ritter all this in his hotel room while he changed clothes for the evening or made drinks, his Airedales sleeping and pacing about. Stretched casually across the bed, her purple dress tastefully flattering, she would sculpt the story carefully, appearing kind without sacrificing humor.

≈

Dana thought Tim was an asshole. She lit a cigarette in the kitchen in front of Uncle Scofield and threw the match in the sink. "Men are," she said.

"Is that right?" Uncle Scofield said.

Dana looked about for an ashtray, then tapped her cigarette on a dirty lunch plate. Men liked Dana. She had long, wavy black hair, heavy breasts and thighs born of the earth's natural pillows—beds of pine needles; watery gulfs without boulders, glaciers, or coral; snow-drifts against rabbit warrens; cool mud banks in the night, empty of hippos, rhinos, and elephants—she was turned soil, winking her seedless rows. She wore flannel shirts partly unbuttoned, the lick of her cleavage dipping into an undershirt with a tiny wrinkled bow.

In the kitchen she sat in a chair with her boots hooked in the rungs under her and her knees wide apart like a man's. She asked me if I wanted to go upstairs to look over the music for tomorrow's re-hearsal, and she was so confident and funny, tickling the filter of her cigarette with her tongue when Uncle Scofield's back was turned, that there was no saying no. There was never any saying no to Dana; I had never tried it because I knew what would happen: nothing. Nothing would happen, and I would go back to being alone and bored, a wallflower, sneaking the dogs Darcy and Ben into my room so I could wake up at night when they shook the bed with their REM. "Look over the music" was a joke not just because Dana never practiced her tuba and was in band only because her friends were, but because men were assholes. She believed they occupied themselves with abstractions such as music, literature, philosophy, economics, and math because they thought they were immortal, which was easy to do since their bodies did not remind them of their mortality. On the other hand, women couldn't escape it. Once a month they felt God twist their guts with a hairpin. Once a month their bodies reminded them of the hideousness of birth. Men's only mortality-reminder was the army. Boot camp and war made them face pain and death, but really few of them went into the armed forces and fewer saw combat. The service was such a paternalistic power-orgy anyway that it didn't really count. Since women were already oppressed by their own flesh, and men were not, it followed that women submitted to the male flesh tool, which impaled them and put them through the hell of love and childbirth. Dana herself had had two abortions. It seemed women's only choice to free themselves was to become more manlike—a mistake. When she met me, she could see that I walked that deceitful path, obsessed with music and death, which was one reason why she hated me at first. The only way I could escape the tyranny of flesh was to embrace what I was—a mortal woman.

"Yuck, my cigarette is all wet. I nigger-lipped it," Dana said. She flicked the whole thing into the sink, where Uncle Scofield picked it up and put it out under the faucet.

"Lipped it, hell, you *licked* it," I said. I was learning Dana's way to keep secrets—to flaunt the truth until no one believed it. Dana hid nothing, and no one could figure her out. She also paraded everyone else's intimacies, which kept people at once safe and unnerved. "C'mon, you whore," she said to me. "Let's go to your room and do bad girl stuff," she said, brushing past Uncle Scofield. It was a good thing he liked her, or Aunt Marge would never even let her in the house.

~

Marge sat on Ritter's hotel bed feeling uncomfortably nude, even though she wore a fairly substantial negligee—a long gulp of burgundy silk with tasteful lace insets. She watched Ritter, who stood absently naked at the bathroom mirror, erratically cutting his own hair.

"I just wish you had been open about these squadrons of other women," she said.

"Possessiveness bugs me, Marge," Ritter said. He put down the scissors.

She really had no reason to be upset. If she could be a two-timer, it followed that either one of them could be a three-, nine-, or ninety-timer. Still, there was something bitter in the discovery that another woman planned to spend the weekend sucking his toes. Since she was disappointed, she must have expected something.

"I don't know what I expected," she said to Ritter, who leaned close to the mirror to clip his eyebrows. He propped himself with his hips against the sink, crushing his penis. In another mood, she would have asked him what it was like to have a penis and to squash it against cold porcelain. Apparently it didn't hurt. He began snipping at his nose hair. "Lovely," Marge said. She realized she must have expected their familiarity and confidences to weave into some kind of constant support, a small, secret hammock to cradle her sleepily in her old age.

"I have no real choice, Marge," he said, stopping the sink and filling it with warm water. She was with him when he picked up the telegram that said Cindy would join him at the hotel in Baltimore at nine. Cindy was on her way. "She miscarried, and it was my baby. She's upset. Am I supposed to stuff her back in a cab and send her off to a Howard Johnson's?"

Somehow, he always did the right thing. He had a point—in a way, it would be selfish of her to keep him from Cindy under the circumstances. He assured Marge he would rather be with her and promised he wouldn't sleep with Cindy. He started to shave.

"You don't shave for me," she said. "Are you going to shower for her too?"

"I'm going to shower for *you*." He smiled through his shaving cream. "We have until nine."

∽

I lay naked on my stomach on the bedroom floor, and Dana straddled my buttocks, massaging my shoulders. She asked me why I ever let her kiss me in the first place, and I said that I was the one who kissed her first, and she pinched me in the neck until I got a cramp. I said I honestly didn't remember, so she rubbed the cramp away. We were cold, and we draped a blanket over us so that with Dana sitting up on my back we had a kind of tepee. It was dark under there, and darkness with the distant sound of a television made us talk, but still I couldn't think of how to tell her why I let her kiss me. I thought of telling her I loved her from the beginning, but we both knew that wasn't true until she first licked me and brought my life back into all my cells strong. There was no death anymore. My body was joy. "Dana," I begged her after school, "Dana, Dana, let's go to your car *now*." I wasn't always sure what she got out of being with me all those weekends, all the bright winter afternoons in her car in the middle of the abandoned K Mart parking lot. She said if I weren't so short and stubby I could be a model, one of the most despicable and pitiful of women, slaves to their skin and to men. She said I did well in music out of a suppressed desire to please men, to be a daddy's girl. But still, we had a lot in common; we had dark secrets to share. We both had carpet-burn scars at the bases of our spines. I told her about my baby and Mr. Dheil, showed her the few letters he sent me, told her about the time when I was eleven and Mr. Dheil caught me bringing a jackknife to bed and got so mad and scared he wanted to hit me but was afraid of making a bruise. My punishment would be that he would stab himself in the arm because I had wanted to hurt him, but I stopped him by saying I had meant to slit my own wrists while he was on top of me, which was somewhat true: I wasn't really sure what I was going to do. Then, he sat down naked on the rug, the old musician who had once toured Europe as a pianist, played flügelhorn for Billie Tyler, sat next to Jean-Pierre Rampal at a banquet in Seattle, and he took the knife and peeled the skin off the tips of the four fingers of his left hand. When I came to my lesson the next week, everything was as before except that he wore bandages and I worshiped him.

Dana told me about her boyfriends, her brother, her abortions, and her younger sister Sharon, who died of leukemia at eight years old. "She was going to be a pretty little tart like you," Dana said, rubbing the backs of my legs. "That's why I love you—I miss my Shadow." She said sometimes she dreamt that she opened her eyes to see Sharon sitting on her bed, healthy, smiling.

"I bet it's not a dream," I said.

≈

"Be a good uncle and take your bath," Dana says. She speaks and walks in Scofield's imagination, taking her haughty time leading him through his house to the upstairs bathroom. She smiles over her shoulder, and her plump thighs wiggle under the requisite French maid outfit she has squeezed on. She swings a key in front of him. "Feel dirty?" she says. "Bath time." The sound of running water comes unusually loud from behind the closed bathroom door.

Unexpectedly, Dana lifts her skirt and drops the key chain into her split-crotch panties. The key itself dangles between her legs through the split. She asks for the magic word. He says, "Please"; he says every three-, four-, and five-letter word he knows, and water streams under the door and down the stairs. He seems to be on the wrong track because the girl smirks every time. She says, "No, guess again," making him want to hold her against the wall and punch the black eyeliner off her face. He knows that if he touches her, her cunt will swallow up the key and he'll have to cut her open to get it.

"Why did you tell your wife? If you hadn't, maybe you'd know the word."

He tells Dana that he has a right to the privilege he seeks; he has paid money for Cam. "No, no, no," Dana says, shaking her head at how funny he is. "You don't want to go in the bathroom anyway." Water squirts around the edges of the door.

"She'll drown!" he cries. "My God! Cam!"

The key appears in his hand.

"That's it," Dana says cheerfully.

"Which word was it?"

She tells him to open the door and he'll find out. He opens it, and inside there is no water, but on the bath mat lies the tiniest baby Scofield has ever seen, about as small and unformed as a newborn kitten.

"Whack yourself out," Dana says.

∼

"My girl can drag as long as she wants," Dana said, and smacked Tread's hand away from the joint I held. I was going to stay the night at Dana's, so I felt loose. After a couple of months, everybody knew it: I was Dana's girl, and whatever it meant, people left me alone.

Tread, Mark, Dana, and I always hung out together, and we sat together at parties. This party was crowded mostly with college kids, some in black clothes and black makeup, some in rag-wool ski sweaters, some, like us, in flannel shirts. A tall, blond-haired boy, who clearly had an audience of other tall, blond-haired boys, brought me a plastic cup of beer and asked me to dance. None of us seemed to know him.

"Do you want some of this joint? Is that it?" I said, offering it to him. While he smoked, I mentioned the fact that no one else was dancing.

"Do you wanna dance?" Dana mimicked him. "Bad lines don't work on her. Bet you'd like to know what would."

He said, "Sure," with a shrug and such a nice smile that I wanted to stop Dana. She said she'd show him what worked on me, and kissed me so hard I spilled the beer he gave me down my boot. The blond boy said, "Whoa," and Tread, who always laughed way too hard whenever Dana kissed me, cackled. In case anyone thought Dana was joking, she stroked my breast and told the boy I wasn't wearing a bra.

"Here's your toke back," the boy said, sliding up alongside me and exhaling the smoke, which I shotgunned from his mouth. I took the toke from him, blinking rapidly because I wasn't sure I liked Dana shocking him that much. People whooped, from where I couldn't tell anymore, and Tread wasn't going to stop giggling for a while, wiping his nose on the back of his hand.

Mark, who never laughed when he was high, said, "She's only fourteen, man." He and the boy spoke seriously about how I was only a high school freshman in band, where we all met, and how Dana and I really were always like that. I felt I shouldn't speak. Dana had set me too far apart, made me mysterious, beautiful, valuable.

The next day Mr. Dombrowski took me aside to talk to me about my future. Dana and her kind were not good for it. Such a drastic change in my behavior so early—I was just a freshman—could mean my demise. I didn't answer; Dana said just because an adult speaks to you and expects a response does not mean you have to give one. Likewise, just because a man stands close and touches your palm doesn't mean you can't walk away.

Mr. Dombrowski told me how he had plans for me: he wanted to make me section leader next year—few sophomores became section leaders—he expected me to be first chair by junior year, and drum majorette my senior year. He knew all these things mattered to me, but I would lose them if I kept being irresponsible. He couldn't know that Mr. Dheil had said the same kinds of things to me. Mr. Terrence, the junior high typing teacher, used to come over during my flute lessons to find me waiting for him on the bed, artificially lubricated. He walked in and undressed, already wiping tears off his cheeks, and he took me in his arms, kissed my head, and let his nose run, and I cried too, and crying he kept saying, "Poor, poor little girl." But by the time I moved away from town, I had grown to hate Mr. Terrence. I finally preferred Kyle's dark variety, Kyle who used to scare me but made me feel professional with his hips slapping my bottom like a mechanical bull. Sometimes Kyle had me in ways that made it hard to breathe—my neck bent or my throat clogged with mucus—and I couldn't help fighting, which made me a "tough calf to brand." It wasn't long before I learned to fight while I could still breathe. Dana, when I told her, said that most rape victims found dead were not intentionally murdered but accidentally suffocated. It was still homicide. She wondered how many hundreds of times I had been raped, and decided that I was a national hero, just nobody knew it.

Mr. Dombrowski could not know that Dana thought I was a hero, or that when she took her clothes off she was shy. We lay on the floor on a soft blanket, and she trailed her fingers over my face, my arm, then my breast, and I touched her, saw the faint ridges of stretch marks on her heavy breasts, the bruises on her thighs she said would never go away, and when she touched herself, I held her till she came. I touched myself too, but usually pretended to come; since I started seeing Dana, I had been masturbating so much that I couldn't always climax. I missed things like Kyle's hips or Mr. Dheil's gray-haired shoulder pushing into my chin, things that told me perhaps I really was an adult, I really was desirable, that I had artistic talent, that I really would play one day for the New York Philharmonic.

I said, "Dana takes good care of me, Mr. Dombrowski; I'm just losing interest in music. It's probably just a stage."

≈

At nine-thirty Marge sat in her room with her German shepherds, Grethel and Mathilde. Restless but used to close quarters, they paced around the twin beds. They would do poorly in the next day's novice trials, and even worse in breed competition. Marge had spent too little time preparing for dog shows lately, going to them indiscriminately, big and little, up and down the East Coast, and for all the cost and travel, she had made few connections, sold few dogs. She picked up the phone and called home.

"Uncle Scofield's out," Cam said when she heard Marge's hello.

Marge felt suddenly impetuous, and invited Cam out to Baltimore. "I'll wire you money. I don't know why I didn't think of this before. We should spend more time together."

"You're never home."

Marge pointed out that Cam spent all her time with Dana. A trip to Baltimore would do her good. Besides, she was in fact a third cousin, family, and family should do fun things together. She would learn a lot at the dog show.

Cam said she had plans for the weekend.

Marge hung up the phone, sat down on the floor, and pulled the seventy-pound Grethel onto her lap. She thought she might cry into the dog's dense coat, but didn't. She had made sure Ritter had no time to wash her smell off his skin, and, when she saw that the hotel towels hung in front of the toilet, she wiped lipstick on each corner of one towel. Spite put potholes in the road of time, and if Marge couldn't be sorry for hurting Cindy, at least she was sorry for vandalizing her own peace.

All through these months with Ritter, she had maintained her presence of mind, independence, and skepticism, but she had somehow let every other element of her life slide. She was going to have to sell dogs, lots of them, for dirt cheap. She would end up unloading them on pet shops, like a puppy-mill breeder. In fact, a puppy mill is largely what K-9 City had become, and that was her fault. She bred the dogs too frequently and carelessly.

And Camille had moved into the house, made herself a home, started friendships with other kids, almost without wasting an hour. At least she hadn't wasted any of Marge's hours. That poor wayward girl with her black T-shirts stinking of cigarettes needed a mother. Marge packed up the dogs and was home again before midnight, despite the boisterous rain.

~

I came back to my room to find that Dana had turned off all the lights but the little one next to my bed, opened the window, and knelt on the floor in front of it, resting her elbows on the sill. "It's gonna rain," she said, without turning her head. Her jeans looked baggy in the ass, and I told her that. I knelt next to her, and she said she was going to sell her tuba.

"Why?" I said. A damp, cold wind washed over me, and my nipples pinched under my shirt. I pressed them, lightly, against the wood window frame.

Dana said she just wanted money, just to have it. We talked about quick ways to get money, especially prostitution. She asked me if I would ever do it again.

I said I didn't think of it as prostitution, and I didn't want to do it again.

"Yeah, but you would anyway. I wouldn't, not that there's anything wrong with it." She felt an affinity for prostitutes, although she didn't know any personally, she said, except me.

"Dana," I said, "will you stop with the hooker shit?" She had told enough people about my past that the student body grieved me more than Mr. Dheil ever did. At school, I told her, a boy threw money at me in the hallway, another asked if I'd give head or let him watch us eat each other out, girls' eyes raked me as I passed, teachers looked away from me, and Mr. Dombrowski had nothing to say to me anymore. "And I'm sick of Tread calling me 'lesbie.'"

"We're not lesbians," Dana said. True lesbians only hugged and petted. A sociology book had dispelled for Dana the myth that lesbians went down on each other. The things she and I did together were really heterosexual male things, attempts to objectify and control each other through our genitals. She said she was beginning to doubt our relationship.

We looked out the window for several minutes, and on the black faces of the trees and sky I saw paramedics, my mother's bed stripped of its sheets and mattress pad, Mr. Dheil's face asking me to leave when I came over unexpectedly, my father busily tucking his plane tickets in his brief case, and Uncle Scofield standing in the bathroom doorway saying he was sorry, he didn't know I was in there, staring like a threatened dog. Kneeling next to Dana, I thought for a second I'd burst into tears so hard I'd fall out the window, but then I knew why I wouldn't cry—my memories stemmed from moments that had a body chemical in common, a kind of insta-freeze, and it now piped through my muscles again. I couldn't cry and couldn't help remembering times recorded on the cogni-chemical arrangements. I was about to tell these ideas to Dana, when a barn owl floated silently over the grass like a tissue ghost on a string. We watched it without surprise, and then the sky flashed.

"One Mississippi, two Mississippi, three . . ." Dana said.

"What are you doing?"

"Five Mississippi, si—" and the thunder broke on our ears and shook the house. Dana said that light was instantaneous, but sound traveled a mile a second. If you saw lightning, then counted the seconds until the thunder arrived, you could tell how far away the storm was.

I said I couldn't be a lesbian, because I hated women's bodies, especially their armpits. I hated men's armpits too, but women's more. Dana said she knew what I meant—some were fleshy folds like dead mouths, and the others with hair in them were long-dead mouths with furry mold in the throat.

"Yaaaaaa!" Dana shrieked, and in one sweep lifted her shirt and pushed an armpit in my face. She rolled me on the floor. "Lesbie friends."

I said no.

She said she was serious, we should be lesbians and not lovers. We should just cuddle; genital manipulation was too destructive. She climbed on top of me and held me, and I thought there was no way I'd let myself lose Dana. I breathed over her mouth and nose, and pressed my thigh against her crotch so gently that she didn't notice until she wanted it there. I let my lips brush along her cheek, and up close like that I could see that she was older, a woman. "Dana," I said. She tilted her head like a movie star, which I hated, so I pushed her onto her back, let my weight down on her, and said "Dana" again, forcing the sound through her skin and skull, sending it prying. I pushed my forehead against hers, and we both opened our eyes. She waited.

"Our souls are just an inch or two apart," I said. I wanted them closer. "Dana." The name searched; it stretched an invisible rainbow bridge, an electric arc of breath; it leavened from the back of my head and swelled the room and found someone else lurking in the air; I was terror; "Dana!" I cried with my face to her throat, seeing that I was terrified my whole life—not of being impaled like the girl in sixth grade who fell off a fence onto a post that pierced through her vagina all the way up to her heart, and there she stood—but of dying itself, just dying. "Dana," I said, meaning, this time, that I didn't want to die. The air flashed and Dana started counting and I stuck my tongue

in her mouth and we both counted out loud with my tongue in
Dana's mouth until we laughed and the air cracked and rained hard
and I was opening fainting rolling on top of Dana her legs wrapped
around she says why don't you have a prick? so I take the mouthpiece
off my flute and we breathe on it 'til it's warm and it's my silvery-
slick cock and I hold it inside both of us at once and I love Dana
Dana Dana Dana

~

The old house drummed with rain, so when Marge came in the
back door, she couldn't tell whether or not Cam was still up. She
rubbed her wet head with a dish towel and searched the kitchen for a
note, some sign from Scofield explaining why he and his car were out
this late. "Cammie!" she called, but the rain spattered like handfuls
of gravel against the windows. If the girls were still awake, maybe
Dana would be leaving soon and Cam would be interested in some
late-night girl talk. Marge wondered if there were any scary old
movies on TV and wished there was ice cream in the freezer. She
thought there was a jar of popcorn in the back of the cupboard. She
looked at her watch, and figured by this time Ritter and Cindy were
done with their carnal greetings and now sat talking in a small,
smoky nightclub Ritter somehow already knew well.

Marge searched but could find no popcorn, so she took off her
jacket and went upstairs. In the open doorway of Cam's room, Marge
paused. She saw Cam and Dana, naked from the waist down.
Propped up on one hand with Dana caged beneath her, Cam stared
up at Marge. Slowly, without looking away, she pulled her other
hand from under her, slid something shiny across the floor, and rolled
it under the bed.

"Get up! Get dressed," Marge shouted. "How dare you?"

Dana stood up, and, with defiance parading as dignity, marched
her bare ass and black bush across the room, where her pants lay
twisted and wet under the open window.

Twice in one night people she loved had cheated on her, Marge
thought, because suddenly she realized she loved Cam. The affection
was unexpected, and the betrayal real. This little girl, to Marge now
her flesh-and-bone daughter, defiled herself in Marge's house with a
seedy, immoral, dull-witted trollop.

"You should know better," Marge seethed at Dana. "An adult," she spat. It occurred to her that what she just witnessed was prosecutable by law. "Corrupting a minor."

Cam had crawled between her nightstand and bed, and cringed there.

"She was corrupted long before I ever got to her," Dana said, zipping up her pants. She turned to shut the window.

"Don't you touch my house!" Marge's body was a great black bear, an animal strange and terrifying to her, fast on its hind legs, its arm heavy and its claws dagger-edged as Dana reeled against the music stand. Paper fell in loud sheets of snow, rain curtained in like diamonds of all sizes, and Dana was running down the stairs. In a burst the strength had come and gone, leaving Marge to stagger shouting after Dana, who crashed out the front door. Marge stood on the front step, her throat raw, still saying, "Get *out!*" and she watched Dana hobble rapidly on the gravel, barefoot with her shoes in her hands, and disappear from the lamplight as she reached her car.

Then, out of nowhere, Cam was running barefoot across the stones, awkwardly, the rain flattening her thick hair, flattening her white shirt against her, glistening on her bare running hips, and in the dark Dana's invisible car door slammed shut and the red taillights opened and glowered and growled, and the rain roared in the trees while the red lights shrank before Cam's white shirt and outstretched arms, and the small red eyes turned onto the street and disappeared. She shouted, "Dana . . . Danaaaa!"

The rain blew on Marge in wet sneezes, and she wept into it because it was cold. "Cammie," she said, "you'll get sick." She called her again, wanting her to pick her bruise-footed way back, drowned bunny, and burrow into Marge's arms. Cam was, from where Marge stood, just a white shirt hanging in the driveway, which suddenly dropped and crumpled hunchbacked on the ground. Marge ran out and gathered up Cam, whose muscles were limp with hate.

Marge dragged her, cursing her, into the house and laid her on the couch. She dried herself and Cam and found them both warm robes.

Cam's eyes focused blankly inward. "Hate you," she whispered.

The girl's hatred made such transparent sense that Marge felt a renewed peace, a purpose. "How 'bout some tea with a little brandy in it?"

Cam refused it, which Marge saw as promising, since she didn't expect a response. In the silence Marge saw again the image of Cam, half-naked, pinning Dana to the floor like a man. She saw a shiny cylinder roll under the bed. She grabbed Cam's knee and pinched it hard. "Okay," she said. "Talk."

/ f / o / u / r /

and
there
she
stood

After practice, I found myself carefully massaging each key of my flute with my dad's old handkerchief, more so than I usually did, thinking I must be about to get my period, since I felt slow and weepy. Dana was absent, and the big news in band that day was that over the weekend someone had broken in and stolen her tuba. Mr. Dombrowski came out of his office and sat next to me while I finished packing up my flute, and we watched the last few stragglers, one boy tying snares, another staggering through the waist-high forest of folding chairs and music stands, and a girl practicing some mysterious part on her baritone sax, and after a moment I heard in it the theme of the piece the saxes were using for All-State auditions. "You think I should try out for All-State?" I said.

"I got the music," he said. "Give it a go." He got up and went back into his office. The one boy beat out the cadence from football season on the snare drum he just repaired. I put my face in my hands, even though I knew I'd make mascara dust around my eyes, but I had an English paper to write on something I hadn't read, I had flunked a math test, and I hated my history teacher, who didn't know how to ask a fair question. My father had called the night before and said a business trip would bring him east in April, his first chance to see me since he left last summer, and he'd have a woman with him he wanted me to meet. I made a mental list of all the work I had that week, and if I wanted to get it done right, I couldn't see Dana till Friday, couldn't play with Ben, and could play my flute only during study breaks. I wondered if in music school you studied only during flute breaks. Somehow, I liked being so busy as to be dead to Dana. It was okay with me if she stole a horn and left me alone to smile at Mr. Dombrowski with my sweat smearing my polished silver, because I had a makeup spelling test to prepare for—being this busy made me feel detached, as if I were in a casket. I could hear Mr. Dombrowski explaining to me about All-State, hear the katzenjammer of the snare and sax, hear in my mind how Dana had done something big, beyond me.

I felt like betraying Dana by talking to Mr. Dombrowski the way I used to, the way I did before I joined Dana's side in the war. Mr. Dombrowski lumped her among the "anti-intellectuals" he battled every day. When we all giggled and passed notes and missed cues during rehearsal, he'd turn to his assistant and say, "Roll in the think tanks; mow them all down." He lifted his hands as though resting them on some low roof over our heads, said we'd never rise with so much holding us down.

He sat down next to me and dropped a thin stack of music in my lap. "The only trouble you'll really have with this piece is in these ten bars here," he said. I looked, and he was right—I couldn't move my fingers that fast. He slapped his knee to keep time and tried to sing the part: "dadada-dididididididididi-da dit daa . . ."

"I miss my mom," I said without thinking. He said he hadn't known me for long, didn't know me very well, and on his own tried to recall the things I had told him about my family. He said not even a year had passed since my mother died, and wasn't it natural, even a good thing, that I missed her. He went on about how parents shape children so much that the children always have their parents with them because in some sense they *are* their parents, and I wanted to tell him that I lied about missing her because we never really liked each other, that she hardly talked to me or looked at me, that she was weak and repulsive, that I didn't miss her because she haunted me, and the truth was I couldn't shake her off.

"I miss my dad too," I said, because with all his talk about parents it seemed the right thing to say. Then Mr. Dombrowski, who rarely smiled, got a warm, bleary look on his face, and said aunts and uncles could be good parents. I didn't know why he was bothering himself over me, so I grabbed up the music and left, afraid he was going to try to hug me. As I headed for the late bus, I nearly ran back to ask him if he was Catholic—all this time he'd been reminding me of that priest, Father Robert, who hung around about the time Grandmom died, and I only just then realized it.

∾

"Get in the tub!" Scofield says, but the baby slips out of his blistered fingers and runs like some kind of deformed elf toward the staircase and down, smearing handprints of flame along the wall.

"I hate you. I'm going to tell," the little voice says, and Scofield takes a deep breath and runs into the flames, but the stairs have quickly burned through and he falls all the way into the cool, damp basement.

He rests there a minute, his own pulse knocking in his ears, and then hears his dogs outside burst into a squealing roar as the flaming creature nears them. "Not the dogs," he says, already crying. "Not my dogs." He runs for the stone steps that lead from the basement to the backyard, but all of the dark is Barghest. The dark sparkles with the gleam of wet noses and eyes, and yet there are no eyes or noses. The dark is a thick, oily black pelt without fur or form; the tail, nothing but a wind, lashes at the backs of his legs; the basement itself is the wide, cold, wet mouth, and the humid floor lifts him, slides him along the ridged palate, squeezes him down the throat. Far away, through the thunder of flames, his dogs scream like puppies.

∾

In the evening in the bedroom, Marge packed the last of four suitcases, instead of her usual one. She always knew something was too thick or murky, twisted about Camille, but she passed it off as teenage melodrama, depression, surging hormones. A week before, that girl had sat in her robe on the couch in the middle of the night, heavy hair tangled in wet cords, sipping a mug of cool tea, and said, "When you love somebody, you have sex for them. Dana and I are blood sisters." She said she was sorry Marge had to see what she saw, but sex was the truth of everything.

Marge turned sideways on the couch to face her and said, "Neither of us is that stupid." She wanted facts, details, dates. "When did you start having sex?"

"I was nine," Cam said.

Marge watched her more than listened to her, watched her hands gesture with their chipped blue nail polish and bitten-back cuticles, her smooth jaw, her face smeared under the garish makeup little girls choose. The voice, helplessly musical, and the words it spoke reeled cellophane movies across Marge's eyes, so that she saw Cam sitting there, and at the same time saw little Cam naked under an old man. And she saw Cam, not so long ago, crying in a hotel bed, "Can we go back to the doctor yet?" waiting for her water to break and the kicking of her poisoned fetus to stop.

Marge wondered what was wrong with her, why she sat riveted, listening to Cam, watching, when she didn't want to hear any more, when it had gone far beyond the possibility of lies into fiction, a horrific fantasy that had been told before, told to Timmy, to Dana, embellished with well-placed details that tapped on the nerve of significance, well-timed tremolos in the voice. Her own jaw and forehead grew rock-hard, and she ground her teeth. Camille *knew.* Cool and wise, she sat apart, as though embroidering the atrocities on a cloth in her lap. Her words rose like blunt needles, then fell on Marge's ear as if parting fibers, pushing through, pulling the prickly yarn behind. Cam admired her work at arm's length; she stroked her stitches, the loops, lazy daisy, padded satin, turkey, French knot. The colors were ivories, peaches, corals, reds, with small but subtly placed blocks of purples, blues, black. The work was alive with wonder, vivacity, and a desperation to survive, and yet nothing sounded more dead. Cam spoke of her mother and grandmother as if the two had died together, were interchangeable, seemingly using her mother as a symbol for both of them. She said she viewed symphonic band and her friends as mere distractions from what really mattered, joining her mother.

"You have to die to do that," Marge said.

Cam insisted it was all the same, and she explained how spirits continued to exist everywhere they ever were when alive. People should spend most of their lives in their favorite places, because then that's where they'll spend most of their eternity. That's what was wrong with war and jail—people trapped in nightmarish places were trapped forever. Marge would forever be with dogs, she with music. Cam regretted her mother hadn't hugged her much, so she could carry around the strong presence of her mother's touch. Now that she had lived in this house some months, she would always be here; her flute would always sound against the walls, even if the walls fell away; her music was caught here in these box shapes, a continuum of time defying the changes in space.

She figured that that was why religious people sanctified certain places and things. Her grandmother had a saint's relic, a splinter of bone she paid quite a bit of money for. "Jesus always walks this earth," Cam said, and her face flushed. She admitted she was afraid of Jesus. All she knew of him was too much love, a grotesquerie. She paused and searched Marge's eyes for some approval of her handiwork so far, for some response to the stitching of Jesus, a wild dark man with woolly black hair and shiny bare muscles, loin cloth tight over genitals the shape and dimensions of an olive tree.

Marge stared. She smoothed her skirt where she'd been crushing it in her fist, and the fabric felt damp against her thigh. Cam hated Jesus in a way, not entirely, but he seemed so self-assured, didn't Marge think, his breakdowns and fears were staged—Gethsemane was a public image ploy. For instance, on the cross he never doubted. On the cross, with hands and feet nailed, if you relax and hang there you can't breathe. You have to push up on the nails through your feet to expand your chest. The crucifixes always show him hanging, not pushing up, and yet he's almost always depicted alive and in some form of passion. Practically speaking, a real man would have doubted, panicked, and suffocated in that position. Jesus was an image-maker, a hoax.

Marge wanted to say something of guidance, something that would lead Cam out of her self-serving absurdity onto a path of reform. The topic was inviting Marge to finish the conversation with unity, transcendence, reprimand.

But the opportunity passed a silent Marge. She would, according to Cam's philosophy, sit forever quiet on the couch, her rusty sense of

Christian obligation stymied before an adolescent theosophist who practiced lesbianism and harlotry. Marge was stumped, disgusted. There was nothing to say to someone in love with eternity, especially to someone in love with an eternity dominated by an aged music tutor who ran a firstclass brothel of little girls.

Cam looked tired. She finished her cold tea and coughed on the leaf bits. She spoke again of her mother's ghost, and Marge cast for a line of thought that would characterize, label, answer the girl. Her mind rattled over the scraps of psychology learned years ago in college and supplemented since by talk shows. Nothing suited. If Cam were a dog she would turn her over to Scofield. "Here," she would say, holding out the leash the way Ritter did when he relinquished his puppy Ben, and Scofield would arrange the choke high on the neck, and Cam would gag her way to a perfect semblance of tractablity and decorum. And yet when Marge looked at her, really looked at her lips, her round, hard breasts like two baseballs, she almost feared Cam would touch her, invite her to drink from the corners of her lips. Sex was all over Camille—she made love to her own voice, when she moved she made love to her clothes, the draught of her breath brought the air near climax, her music was the mastery of sex.

Marge sent her to bed, then looked around the living room. Perhaps it was just because she was so tired, distraught first over Ritter—now nearly forgotten—or because it was so late at night, but the room looked different. She put a coat on over her robe and went out to look at her dogs. She knelt next to her old German shepherd, who seven years ago had won his Utility Dog title. Vaguely, she could remember training him. The kennel smelled different. Everything was different.

~

After school on Wednesday, Dana's car was parked at the curb right behind my bus. I got in with her, embarrassed by my armload of books, all neatly covered with brown paper. She looked as though she'd had a makeover, her hair trimmed and blown dry with a round brush and her pimples barely noticeable under foundation.

"Tony's brother's back," she said, so I didn't have to say anything as we pulled past the bus and someone I didn't know leaned out the window to shout, "Yo, Dana!"

I dumped my books on the floor at my feet, and she told me again that the bottom of the car was rusted and could break through, and I said so fucking what. I didn't even look at her. She said the weather was so nice they thought they'd get some people together to go canoeing, and that's why she picked me up. I said I had homework, obviously. I wondered to myself who these people canoeing on a balmy January weekday afternoon might be, breaking ice on the river banks with their paddles, getting their down jackets wet, people in their twenties not studying, not working.

"We were going to go earlier, but we waited for you," she said. I saw them sitting around their bongs a few extra hours to wait for a high school freshman. Something told me none of us would go canoeing. In fact, when we got to Tony's house, the gang had called the canoe rental and found it was closed for the winter.

I had never met Tony's brother Andy before, and he was not tall, but solid-bodied, with his shirt open over a smooth, hairless chest. Andy's two friends said hi to me, no one smoked or drank beer, and the room smelled of coffee. Dana fell on the couch next to Andy, and I sat next to her on the floor. Andy and Dana didn't kiss but sat so much against each other that I knew they slept together. We talked an hour and watched the news, and Andy's friends got up to leave. They worked for a moving company and worked weekends too, so they occasionally got a weekday off. Tony came in the front door and ran right up the stairs. Everyone said, "Hi, Tony," but he didn't answer. It was decided that the guys would give me a ride home, and Dana walked me out to their car.

"You could have talked more," Dana said.

I said I didn't know anybody.

"You always talk."

"I talk to you," I said. "I only talk to you, Dana."

≈

Late the next morning when Marge woke, she squirmed in her bed, in her body, for the things she knew. While she sat alone in the kitchen with an empty coffee cup, Scofield walked in and asked what she and Cam were talking about when he came home last night. "Girl stuff," Marge said, knowing Scofield would simply shrug and continue his search for the marmalade.

Over the next few days, a fear replaced the hate and pity that warred in Marge over the sight of the girl. Marge saw her sitting at their dinner table using a fork to squeeze the beans out of cooked green bean pods, playing in the mud-slushy yard with Darcy and Ben, doing her homework at the coffee table because her own desk was too messy. Marge found herself sitting on the back porch in the cold when she should have been working the dogs, grooming them, or doing the books, just staring, like someone spinning her car's wheels in the mud, knowing it won't move, deciding to stay in the car and listen to the radio for the first time in years instead of putting chains on the tires or stuffing a blanket under them or going for help. Shivering on the back porch, she avoided tears over the thought of a young child raped and ruined, then fended off fury over the way the story was told, the way it wound up neatly—"And here I am"—the way Cam's life went on as before, placidly, icily. Marge had compassionate thoughts: the poor girl had found her mother's dead body, she's still in shock. And she had more and more irrational ones: her mother died in her arms and sucked the soul out of this child and blew a demon into its place. The pity and hate gave way to fear, fear of perversions, of the unnatural, of someone who has been someplace no human should go—and liked it—such as an airless, lifeless planet, or the deepest, body-crushing ocean bed, or the leech-filled bottom of a cave many miles deep. Cam not only had gone to some place of this sort, but had lived there, gotten familiar with its fantastic, alien creatures, felt at home in the black and inimical terrain. Now she walked in Marge's world a stranger, and she poisoned it with the exhalation from her very pores.

Scofield came looking for Marge one night and found her with her last suitcase packed. "Foster parents go through screening," she said, opening and slamming her empty drawers one last time. "They go through years of counseling before they take on a child like this." Scofield folded his arms, disappointed in her, reasonable, stronger. "And besides, they *want* the children," she said.

They sat on the bed together, and she told him that she had spoken with her lawyer, and K-9 City would remain. She'd board most of her dogs with him. Scofield shook his head and got up to pace the room. He glared at her, his mouth opening to protest, then closing with something more than rage, dread, or wounded pride. Since he wouldn't speak, Marge told him about Ritter, and her plans to stay with him. Finally Scofield asked her what it was about this girl that was driving his wife away from him. His face was pleading, but awash with a smile of disbelief.

Scofield sat down on a wooden chair draped with several layers of his laundry. Marge, having said all she had to say about her lawyer and her plans for her dogs, fell silent. He had not reacted to her clipped confession about Ritter, whom she felt suddenly proud of, and now she waited, confused and nervous, knowing how he could explode, strike her, but also seeing how tired and old he looked, his head bent toward the floor where a penny lay near-buried in the rug, his hands wrinkled and grayed with newspaper ink, his legs tilted awkwardly, lifelessly.

"Don't leave me alone with her," was all he said.

Marge smiled. She felt strong from the compassion that surges in the decided betrayer. "You're the disciplinarian. A self-made man. You tame anything."

Scofield looked back at the coin in the rug and said nothing more. Marge, aware now of an unexpected talent for the appropriate, got herself ready for bed in the guest room.

In the middle of the night, Scofield stuck his drunken head in the door and hissed a gust of cool alcohol breath—"Fuck you then, and take the damn barghest with you"—and Marge inhaled his exhaust and anger, waiting tensely in the dark while he shut the door as quietly as he could, as though he believed she slept, and the crack of hallway light narrowed around his great bobbing head until she was alone again in the blackness, wondering whether she really understood him any better when he was sober; he seemed to Marge to have allowed certain parts of his life to overgrow; unkempt, they pinched and swallowed up the paths the two of them used to reach each other, so that when he spoke, sober or not, the words crashed into the weeds and vines and left nothing more than sound and flutter, telling her only that some strange animal moved in there. She worried that maybe somehow he couldn't be trusted with Cam, certainly he couldn't handle the girl's past any better than she could, and maybe he'd have something like a nervous breakdown because she left, but Marge had no time for misgivings now, her wheels were on solid pavement; she had already spent too much time thinking. She couldn't sleep. She propped herself up on another pillow, turned on the light, and pulled an old pocket novel out of the night table drawer.

～

Scofield wakes on the couch to the sound of Marge dragging suitcases out the back door. He has a headache, he's thirsty, and his mouth feels as though he swallowed sewage. He wonders what it is he did swallow, and the coffee table shows several new rings on its surface, and one guilty, empty glass. Scotch. When Marge comes back in and hurries up the stairs, he pisses in the downstairs bathroom, then peeks out one of the back windows. Marge has, by herself, attached her car to the back of the mobile home, which is turned toward the driveway, ready to head down the road.

Scofield lies back on the couch. Before he drinks three glasses of water, before he takes aspirin and showers, he wants Marge out of the house. To him, she's as good as long gone except for her thumping around, shuffling through drawers, making her stray comments as she passes by him—"I'm going to need furniture." His business will rock, then stabilize. He'll sell off most of the dogs that are there just for show, Marge's dogs. He'll pick up where she left off with the police-dog breeding, which she did too often anyway, driving herself to scramble to keep ads in magazines and make frequent phone calls overseas. Maybe he can fall asleep again, if Marge will just leave.

He hears Cam's voice upstairs asking Marge what she's doing.

"I'm moving out," Marge says, in a voice that invites no questions. He hates her, he's always hated her; she's never been anything more than someone who seemed to have interests similar to his. Her interests and ideas were always skirting his, never quite overlapping enough, never quite as convinced, as definitive. Her busy activity sometimes looked more like stupidity, an inability or an unwillingness to explore his life and her own. She was useful. He used her. She understood him well. He starts to miss her so much that he feels like crying into the cushions, knowing he's only tired and that Marge is right upstairs sweeping the hallway. He listens to the purposeless swishing until he's about to yell at her to get the hell out of the house already, when Cam comes downstairs, dressed in jeans and primped. She sits on the wing chair and says she's sorry. She feels as though it must be her fault, because he and Aunt Marge were best friends. She leans forward and cries into her own knees. Her back looks narrow under her oversized sweater, and her hair looks fresh, curly, and clean even though he knows she hasn't washed it lately.

He tells her that Aunt Marge found somebody else to be best friends with, and her leaving has nothing to do with Cam. "You're a good kid," he says, and makes her smile.

~

I wanted to talk to Dana. I knew Aunt Marge would be a scorn-wielder and I scorned her back, spited her, watched her do all the wrong things. She never called Dana's mother to tell her what she saw us doing. A good mother would have. A good mother would have talked to me more than once about the things I'd done and would have decided something, grounded me or taken me to some doctor of the body or mind or both. She just kept asking me if I could play my flute someplace else.

I went to school, and when I came home I could see Uncle Scofield out back with a couple of policemen, by the kennel where he kept the dogs that were trained and were for sale. The house was so quiet, I put my coat and books on the floor by the door. I took off my shoes and walked slowly in my socks. I loved the house. Somehow, with Aunt Marge gone, it was mine. Now, I would cook dinners for Uncle Scofield. I would dust the dining room table. Standing in the middle of the living room, I realized how little this house looked like my mother's house, and there was nothing I could do to make it the same. But with Aunt Marge gone, there was room for my mother. She had visited this house years before, and some waft of her spirit must have lingered. I tiptoed up the stairs with my eyes closed, feeling for her ghost. The rooms were especially sunny from a glare off the snow that dusted the lawns. "Mom?" I said. Somewhere, a clock ticked, and the walls creaked from the wind. In my room, I pulled open my nightie drawer, and the sound irritated me so much I wished I were deaf, I wished I had an ice pick to jam in my ears and the world would be silent, I would be closer. I'd at least be free from the voices that rumbled through throats sweating on my throat, never lying to me, telling me the absolute truth. I found my mother's nightgown in its plastic bag and started to open it, figuring maybe she could visit me only in the day, since she probably had been to this house only in the day. But then I was so lonely for her that I knew she wouldn't come. I went to the hall phone and called Dana again.

When she didn't answer her phone, I looked up the other number, her parents'. Her mother answered, and I said I hadn't seen or talked to Dana in two weeks now, and she never answered her phone.

Dana's mom said that she herself had unplugged the phone because it rang too often at all hours. "Dana ran away," she said. With Andy. Dana's mom was going to have Dana's line disconnected.

I tried to keep her on the phone longer, just because it felt as though it were the last connection to Dana, the last connection to a mother, the last person to talk to, but she didn't know anything more about Dana's whereabouts, what she was doing and why. She suspected the two had eloped.

That evening, after the last class had left, Uncle Scofield came in happy. He had sold a patrol/narcotics dog for sixty-five hundred dollars. He went into his office, and when he came out, he got in his car and left. I figured he would come home soon for dinner at six, the way Aunt Marge always had it, so I looked all through the kitchen for something to make, but I couldn't find the cookbooks, and the pans and utensils were not where they would be in my mother's kitchen. Uncle Scofield must have been excited about his sale but still lonely and upset, so I wished I could figure out what to make for dinner, but somehow I couldn't move, couldn't decide anything. When six o'clock arrived, I had two ham and cheese sandwiches made, with potato chips and pickle slices on the side, the way they do in restaurants. I made the sandwiches the way my mother taught me, scrunching up the ham slices like wadded tissues, layering with cheese, lathering one bread slice with mayonnaise and the other with mustard, topping it off with thick, heavily salted and peppered tomato slices. Six o'clock came and went, and I took time to set the dining room table, lining up the place settings just right, laying out the silverware just for show. At eight-thirty I ate both sandwiches.

Wondering almost every minute why I couldn't do anything, knowing I was behind in English, lost in math, and getting low grades in history, I watched television until Uncle Scofield came home at eleven. He kicked my books and coat out of the way to get through the door, looked at me, then kicked them again hard and cursed me. I started to cry unusually loudly, unlike me to cry at all, thinking either I was more upset about Dana than I realized, or this was a smart response to his anger.

I gathered up the books while he took off his coat, and said I was sorry, I meant to put them away. "I made you dinner," I said.

"I ate out."

He drew me by my arms to the couch, asking what I was watching, and we sat down and he held me against him. He smelled the way men smelled at Mr. Dheil's sometimes, with a pure alcohol sweetness on his skin. He started talking right through my TV show, saying things about how he meant to do right by me and how hard it was for the two of us to be on our own. He told me things I couldn't follow about money and a maid and cadaver detection and thirteen grounds for divorce and Aunt Marge's hysterectomy. Aunt Marge had had something wrong, and couldn't carry children. The way I was leaning on him, he seemed small. The hand he rested on his knee looked like any other man's hand, broad, square, scarred with marks peculiar to his trade, the triangular gashes and punctures of dog teeth. He told me about a conversation he had with a friend in a bar that night. The friend's wife had left him with a teenage daughter, and he was full of experiences with lawyers. Divorce proceedings could drag on. Uncle Scofield and I had to learn about each other so that we could survive. He would call my father soon to fill him in, but he would not allow me to be torn out of yet another home.

When the next show came on, neither one of us moved, and we watched it together, cuddled up like that, until we both fell asleep.

∿

Marge sits high in the driver's seat, one foot balanced on the clutch, one fist around the stick shift, even though the engine is off. Looking slender in her sneakers, blue jeans, and sweatshirt, her hair darker than he's ever seen it, she looks divorced already.

Before he can stop himself, he's telling her about a letter from Cam's father, who's getting remarried soon and has offered to take Cam back. Harry jogs past, dressed for school with a sack of books thumping his back. He hollers that he forgot something in the shed and says, "Break a leg, Mrs. Scofield!" which he says before all her shows. Scofield notices a poetic irony in the boy's good will, and so that Marge appreciates it too he points it out with a loud, sarcastic snort. When she doesn't react, he says, "Break a goddamn leg."

Without taking her foot off the clutch, Marge absently sweeps her hair back into a ponytail and fixes it there with a mysteriously appearing rubber band, the way he's seen Cam do. "I've got a long drive," she says.

"Let's send her to Chicago," he says, knowing Marge is not leaving entirely because of Cam, but because she has someplace to go, because she isn't his wife but a stranger who has already left her husband; she's an honored guest sitting there in his yard, her camper and her dogs all honored guests.

She looks down at the keys hanging from the ignition, sad. She's trying to act like Marge, he thinks, and he realizes, with some irritation toward himself, that he would take back the actress, maybe even prefer the actress to the real Marge. She looks past him, over the sideview mirror, past Harry and Cam, who make their way together to Harry's car. "You've changed," she says, and mentions things he's never thought of, how he comes to bed too late at night, how he embarrasses her at parties by talking about God, he takes more and more time off work to watch afternoon television, he never returns peoples' phone calls, he stopped going to his students' matches and shows, he once said she kissed like a man, he refuses to help her raise Cammie, too often he throws "temper tantrums" over things such as an empty cereal box, he spends too much money on booze, he doesn't keep his checkbook, he speaks too slowly, tells the old man Sweeney private things like she wears support hose and calls 900 "true confession" numbers, tears the ruff on her show dogs with choke chains, and refuses to talk to her about anything serious.

"Come down outta there!" he says, and grabs for her arm. "Let's get a cup of coffee or something." But he lets her sit there, seeing her for what she is—a rebellious child, mouthing pitiful, irrational, sentimental crap, a best friend taking her toys and running off, about to leave his sandbox empty of all the best toys, hers, empty of her footprints and sand castles, a scornful bitch who's read too many *Ms.* magazines, filled out too many of those stupid, biased questionnaires—"My partner gives me cunnilingus (a) hungrily; (b) only when I ask for it; (c) occasionally, with reserve; (d) never"—who needs a belt cracked across her ass. "You let him fuck you, didn't you?" he says, and wants to run straight through the camper walls and blast out the other side, sending the whole thing crumbled and toppling.

"I wanted to see what it was like to be awake."

She says it as though she hasn't fucked the man yet, so Scofield says, "I deserved that," as though he didn't want to smash her face bloody and shattered into the windshield. As soon as she starts to cry, almost giving in, saying she doesn't want to leave so many good years behind, Scofield sees her face broken in the windshield glass, her ribs violently displaced by the steering wheel, and he jumps up into the cab, throws her sideways across the seat so her bloodied head raps into the emergency brake, and gropes under her sweatshirt, through the slippery kindling of snapped ribs and steering wheel, and he squeezes her breasts soft under her coarse bra until they nearly burst, and she kicks at his chest and pulls his hair and beard, and he reaches in her pants, hooks his finger in her snatch like a tab on a beer can— if only she would leave—and his pants are open and he comes against her knee.

"You can't just stand there all day," Marge says, and starts the engine, the foot poised over the clutch all this time finally doing its job. She rests her left hand on the door, ready to pull it closed.

"Goddamn slut," he says. "Go."

/f/i/v/e/

millions
of
strange
shadows

Father Robert stopped at the Center, as he did most Friday afternoons. He went in to talk to the receptionist and anyone else who
was only half busy. He liked being there with the women, always
bustling stony-faced, eyes cast with urgent, grim compassion as other
women filed through with bruises and children whose hair had been
pulled out, teeth knocked out, eyes blackened. The phones were
quiet, women hammering numbers into them before they could ring,
and the waiting area was more crowded than usual. A man clutched
two small boys to him, a black woman sat by herself, a dark-haired,
dark-eyed woman held a baby in her lap, and a well-dressed,

coiffured woman sat stiffly beside her daughter, who looked, for an alarming second, just like Cam. She was the same age, had a similar build and short, curly, mousy hair. Her mother absently left her purse open on her lap and stared at the receptionist, who scrawled rapidly on paper with the phone receiver between her ear and shoulder. The girl did not so much look like Cam as she lounged in her chair like her, as though on film, the colors of the room, the light from the window, even the postures of the other clients conspiring to accent her eyes, balance the angle of her arm, the curve of her stomach, the sweep of her thigh. She too stared expectantly at the receptionist, yet posed as though accepting a lover of great aesthetic discernment.

Father Robert stood against one wall, waiting patiently to greet the receptionist. He had not seen much of Cam since her grandmother's funeral, and he thought of her only as he did this afternoon, when he happened across something that reminded him of her. Certain heady, exotic smells reminded him of her house and her family, her mother growing weak and sickly and her grandmother bright-eyed, birdlike, and strong. The shouts of children recalled to him uncomfortably the times he spent leaning over a playground fence to watch her hold back her shirt as she swung upside down on a jungle gym, stand idly while other girls skipped rope, disappear by herself under a bush, pull her coat open to the wind as though trying to fly. Once he saw her showing another girl how to hold a stick like a flute, and, being very exact about where they placed their fingers, they played their stick flutes throughout the recess, sitting on the hard-packed dirt. He stopped visiting the playground after she confronted him. At first he had been pleased when he saw her approach.

"What are you doing here?" she had said dully.

"Seeing how you play." He felt compelled to tell her the whole truth, that her grandmother Anne worried him with her talk of the "sins" of Cam's parents, the tales always vague with a flourish that left credibility slight. He was waiting for some sign that Cam was abused physically or verbally or was simply neglected. He suspected that perhaps Anne herself did things to Cam, given the suspicious way she fretted and theorized over lunches with him in narrow, jumbled, strangely lit diners with pipes along the ceiling fuzzy with dust. Anne was always on the verge of some change, like an adolescent, about to improve her relationship with God, with Cam's father, about to do more to help her daughter cope with her illness, her wooden marriage, her moody child.

"I don't like it anymore," Cam said. She looped her fingers in the chain-link and looked away. "I wish you'd stop coming here. You're Grandmom's friend."

He felt more shamed than beneficent suddenly, as though in his heart he'd been a Peeping Tom, no better than people caught spying on their children while they bathed or teaching them to masturbate so they could watch. "I care about you," he said, wishing it were truer than it was. He wondered how much he really cared for anyone since he was estranged from his own family, now uncountably large with his brothers' children. He distanced himself from peoples' confessions and from the malevolence the Center collected. In order to devote himself to solutions to problems, to give a penance or recommend a therapy, he had to grow callous and rational about the perversions and brutalities. Whereas ten years before he had been impetuous, brokenhearted and hostile toward the outrage of human nature, now he thought no more about mankind's evil than an architect thought about a drafting table. Sin was a given, a constant, not a material of his trade, not something to react against, not even so much something to forgive as it was something to lean his elbows on while he worked.

"I'll stop coming here then," he said, and waited by the fence, and so did she.

She frowned and gripped the fence with both hands. He hoped she would make some request that he be her friend too, that perhaps he could come around to the house more often, some request that would make his interest in her practical, explicable, pious. He prayed over her frown, a wordless, formless prayer, more an ache than a blessing. He reminded himself that all people were his children.

"God has nothing to do with me," she said.

～

Early in the morning, Cam sits eating Pop Tarts still steaming and burning her fingers, as she does every day. Her jeans are tight from being in the dryer, the way she said they'd be when she argued with Scofield about it at the Laundromat after their own dryer broke down. From where he stands at the sink, Scofield can see how uncomfortably tight they are, how they slice behind her knees and above her thighs. The novice K-9 officers have long since arrived; in their several working uniforms—navy blue, sky blue, and khaki—they mill over by the obstacle course, as they will every day, twice a day, for the next twelve weeks, as they have been, for Scofield, for the last twelve years, but he doesn't watch them, he knows they're there, waiting, some of them sending their dogs sloppily over the catwalks and stone-wall jumps, and he watches how Cam's whole leg bounces nervously on her pointed toe, and in the jigging shadow of that thigh, her twat punches a W into the denim. More than to trace lightly the taut crease of her crotch, he wants to feel how it is to have his balls bound likewise in a blue cotton tourniquet and to scratch them delicately through the pulsing fabric. Better yet would be to have her body limp and so thinly, fiercely swaddled as it is and to touch that twice-pouting letter, free from any awareness or reaction of hers. Cramped in her faded blue winding sheet, she sits comfortably, her knee bobbing, her flannel shirt open wide to expose a red snap of tube top, her fingers gone white with propping a history book around her plate of chocolate crumbs. With his eyes fixed on the denim blades cutting into her skin, he thinks they must have slipped through the skin so cleanly as to stop the blood, stop the heart, and leave every cell deliciously still, suspended, warming to rot, invulnerable because now she was just a collection of microscopic objects, the micrography of steak, severed from the conundrum of the rights, the threat, the violation, the kill.

His parts in his pants flush hot and sweat some luscious dampness through his shorts without getting hard, and he feels the skin slacken, so that his balls rest on the rim of the left leg hole, teetering there, ready to fall slowly down his pant leg, a drool of skin, down, down, to bump against the knee, when suddenly Cam's book tips as she lets go with one hand and with one swipe her breasts bulge free to the air, to his eyes, and the history book is saved, her eyes go on reading, her leg goes on incessantly, mechanically jiggling. But her breasts are there, peach-milk roundness swirls and shadows of ovals and white-glazed bowls, and a pink nipple nudges flannel. The lights in the kitchen dim as if some high-voltage engine has clicked on, and her voice sounds, she talks down through the bare speakers of her chest, "The guys are waiting for you."

～

I moved my bed up against the window, with both the sash and the storm window opened all the way even though the temperature had fallen well below ten, and I knelt there, leaning straight and stiff as though in a pew; I could have toppled out like one of those plastic baby dolls with their backs straight and their knees bent for diapering, but the bite of cold air blew me in, held me up, and I played my flute into the rasp of winter branches. I played what I could remember of the *Quatuor pour la fin du temps,* the clarinet solo "Abîme des oiseaux," which was perfect for the long, thin night air, giving me time to adjust my embouchure to the changing breezes and the frost in my flute. As my fingers stiffened and my neck tensed with shivering, I forgot the quartet yet played it still somehow, not pronouncing flute-wise what appeared on the score but echoing into the galaxy the unwritten notes that had vibrated in the composer who slept for years in a morguelike drawer.

If the apocalypse was where the bank of the temporal broke off into the wash of the eternal, then the Dana I knew had broken off, set herself adrift in my mind. For my Dana, there was no more tramping of concrete body parts, her mouth laughing under lip gloss, her fingers a surprise of daintiness, her hair a mat of sprays and stories. No more could her voice march through deliberate requalifications of herself, for to my ears she was silent. Her movements, histories, words, images eddied, sloshed, and would eventually congeal into some solid impression with a label, Dana, to which I could affix "an old friend," "a sister," "a traitor." Dana, she lies on Uncle Scofield's couch, dozing before a black-and-white Saturday afternoon movie, dozing while I'm leaping inside, prancing to talk with her. We wait for Tony after school and laugh at all the fluffchicks and dweebs that go by. "God," Dana says, her face not laughing, not waiting for her hunk Tony anymore, her face not even Dana's anymore, "I'm so bored." Dana hands me a bag of pot while we pull off the road for the cops. "Roll down your window and drop this out," she says. Dana cries on the floor in my room, sitting Indian-style on a rolled-up sweater, because she saw that her father had to read the newspaper by laying it on the floor and standing over it. On a cold Friday night in the stands we watch the game, and Dana's quiet with her arms under the overlay of her band uniform; then she says, "Smell my finger," and I do. One afternoon after rehearsal, she says to Tread and Mark, "Shut up you jerk-offs," because they mentioned a trip the three of them took to the shore without me. With a pocketknife, Mark carves off a piece of his Quaalude for me at a party one Saturday night, and he says he admires me, talks about my dedication to school and music, my ability to get along with all kinds of people, and then he and I do it right there in front of everyone, and soon other couples are doing it too, and he's moving and moving and I'm dizzy, woozy, it goes on and on, sleepy, delicious rises of bottoms and breasts; others just sit and talk, ignoring us all. Mark and I rock on and on, and my lower back chafes against the carpet, and the burning disperses the pleasure so that I pull our shirts up enough to let our stomachs and chests slide skin together, and I love Mark deeply, hug him round, and he says he's always loved me, he'll take care of me, we're mates, and all the couples moan politely, to excite, compliment, brag, and one by one some of us dare to climax audibly, but Mark and I go on sleeping, fusing, and somewhere in the room, with someone, Dana has her own.

I blew air over my flute, a tiny whoosh, and the cold outside made an embouchure of my bedroom window, sounding some sort of silence, breaking my body into particles of eternal noise, and I whirled about the icy room, a vortex of darkness, shape, an absurdity of furniture, empty of souls. Whether God is or isn't, I thought, this is vast. My thoughts crackled blue like lightning, zapping the wide synapse of the room.

≈

Scofield comes upstairs for the night, and the hallway is cold, and he sees that Cam hangs there at the dark end of the hall like death, hangs there in her jeans and T-shirt, and in his own room he can hear the furnace chugging, the room so hot he breaks into a sweat. He belches a sickly belch, sorry he drank as much beer as he did, feels it go on fermenting in his bowels, and as he gets in bed he feels a rush of diarrhea stop short at his sphincter, but he hesitates to go to the bathroom because Cam is hanging in the hallway with Barghest cold all around her. His fear has taken a strange daring, boldly following him into the bright winter mornings where he hides in the woods with his leather tube sleeve on his arm, and when the cop's shepherd takes him, he stands up and kicks at it, shouting in falsetto, "Call 'im off, boss, oh! it hurt it hurt!" And the fear riles him during obedience work, so that the men marvel and he readily knows all the corrections, all the answers to their handling problems without listening to them anymore. A sense of humor ripens in him, and he lets a dog drag him on his back by a jute sleeve as he looks woefully up to heaven and shrieks, "Oh, Lord, Lord, just don' let him bite my black ass," and in his mind he stands back from himself and sees the men laugh at the change in him, even the black Sergeant Corey smiles and shakes his head. The fear tightens his muscles, strengthens them as he lifts Corey's ninety-pound shepherd by the scruff with one arm and the men say, "Man, I wish I had a camera," and when the training's over they don't want to leave.

Scofield is not afraid but brave, and empties his bowels quickly in the hall bathroom. The cold comes not necessarily from Barghest but from Cam's room, and he touches the door, closes his eyes. He bursts in, and his breath clouds his vision in the dark. "It's like a goddamn meat locker in here," he says, and all at once Cam is out of bed, standing in the middle of the room. He shoves her. "Shut the fucking window before the furnace explodes."

Without fumbling or shivering, she lowers the storm window, then shuts and locks the sash. In the light from the hall, in the cold, she is lean and graceful; she is old, a lady. In her pajamas, she turns around and sits cross-legged on the bed. Even though the hall light shines directly in her face, she doesn't squint; she looks right at him. He shrugs. "I just thought something was wrong," he says. "Trying to lower a fever?"

"People can't live in cold like this."

He begins to shiver, and she sits so still he wonders if she's alive at all. He asks her if this latest stunt was done out of sympathy for street people or if she's just terribly inefficient at suicide, but she doesn't answer. Then the cold gets in, mingles with the fear and with the sickness in his stomach, and he leaves her room, stands at the top of the stairs knowing he never sees Barghest when he's looking for it, but there, at the pit of the dark stairwell, at the bottom of the steps, is the round, black face and box muzzle; he looks hard because it could be a pair of shoes, a rumpled coat hovering there in the trick of blackness; he grabs the phone book off the hall table and throws it down the steps, and it lands with a slap, but the image remains, now with a rectangle of yellow pages behind it, and the dog makes its heavy way up the stairs, swaying its great tail, bobbing its massive head, and Scofield holds his head up, holds his breath, closes his eyes as the dog disappears near the top of the steps as it always does; the sickness burns in his organs, rattles through the veins in his upper arms and thighs, charges and cramps his heart; his neck throbs and his eyes tear freely, and he stands there, alive like that.

~

In English class the teacher passed out a blue, hazy ditto with words down the left margin. I hadn't missed one class and was going to ask if there was some mistake, but then I saw everyone else writing on the ditto. A vocabulary quiz.

Asperity.

Cruciform.

Feral.

Gamin. A few weeks had passed since Aunt Marge left. Now that I was Uncle Scofield's new best friend, now that he told me things, called me "Big Sister," I wanted to ask him if he and Aunt Marge were divorced yet, but I didn't want to nag.

Gustatory.

Logotype.

Malapropism.

Mansuetude.

Mnemonic. Mr. Dheil was not married.

Neophyte.

Partake.

Repository.

We were expected to define the words in the spaces provided. On the board the teacher gave us two extra-credit words, encomium and sine qua non. If two people make love and one or both of them is married to someone else, then difficulties arise only if a promise has been broken, a dishonesty perpetrated, or someone tends toward incapacitating jealousy. Adultery was a sin, but fornication didn't seem to be; my grandmother said sin was something you did that caused you stress and confusion, and when you upset yourself, God got angry. I was never stressed or confused. I had seen only a few of the words before and wasn't sure of their meaning. Many of the men who visited Mr. Dheil and me were married. I was married to Mr. Dheil.

Asperity, "great wealth."

Feral, "curly-haired."

Gamin, "willing to go along with things." Dana was married to Andy. Dana probably kept an apartment, an unthinkable thing because I had never shopped, or cleaned, or paid paper with paper, the way my father used to do on Monday evenings. Dana could have eloped with me, but Andy had broad shoulders and a penis, and I knew that no matter what Dana said about men, their shoulders and penises were indispensable to her well-being. She herself had told me that women who had sex with men had healthier minds and bodies than all other women because of the male chemicals they breathed and absorbed through skin and vaginal tissues. Without constant bodily contact with men, women were sickly.

Mansuetude, "serving a man." Dana also said many more women die at the hands of their spouses or lovers than do men, and that one out of three women is raped in her lifetime.

Neophyte, "one who loves new things."

The teacher wrote "5 minutes" on the board. The plastic bag in which I kept my mother's nightgown was crushed on the bottom of my wastepaper basket, and the nightgown lay out on my bed, loosing my mother into the room. First thing in the morning, I had laid out the nightgown and let her vapors go. I had been using it all wrong, trying to use my own olfactory cells to reach her, when the dogs had twenty million times more olfactory cells and seemed unaware of any spirits.

Partake, "to eat the body of Christ."

Repository, "where Christ's body is kept."

Encomium, "a fetal bowel movement."

Sine qua non, "a sign about nothing, a word without meaning."

∾

Cam lives outside the circle of his dog work and his phone calls with Marge, which are more convoluted and resonant than their romance or marriage. He phones her, and the man with a dog's name, Ritter, answers, and Scofield can say, "Put my wife on," because the man has a dog's name and a lower status. Many of Scofield's dogs wear badges and get salaries and are given funerals with flags and trumpets and rifles, and from what he knows of this man, he's despicable, breeding Airedales as though they were crocuses, going for color or curl, eventually just giving the shelters more fur to burn. He calls her with Scotch in his blood, because drunkenness tells Marge more than he could with words—that he's living without her advice, he has other friends, she's not worth calling when sober. He tells her directly tonight why he drinks before talking to her: "This way I don't remember anything you say," which isn't true—he always remembers just enough to give him a reason to call the next night. That she never hangs up on him and even calls him herself once in a while is all he needs, really. His days never included her anyway, and her attachment to him shows him that his existence is not violent or meaningless, that his life is justified by their marrow-and-sap attachment, cuffing and sleeping like two puppies in the woods; they have a shared quiddity, easy and unspoken as siblings' blood. As long as she speaks to him, his place among those with hugs and wristwatches is affirmed.

But tonight he hangs up with abruptness, repelled by her voice, which sounds, somehow, through some quirk of wire and sound waves, as though it could be any woman's voice. The voice suggests that his blood has been quickly displaced in her by Ritter's pump and seed. When he thinks of this man with the decorator dogs sleeping beside Marge, waking up near dawn and parting her lifeless buttocks, he lets the line disconnect without ceremony, and he sits on his couch in the middle of nowhere.

Something tells him there will be no more Barghest to debase him, and a freedom has been granted him, the freedom of those who do not belong. He climbs the stairs in the way Barghest did, on all fours, with disinterested deliberateness, and stands upright at the top, where the dog disappeared for the last time. In Cam's room there is light from the moonless window, light from the walls and the rug, so that he can make out her tiny body on the bed, where she lies motionless and awake, resigned under the square white ceiling. "Don't move," he says, and he is already hard, already coming and rising at the same time, and he does what he has already done countless times, living out the commonplace, ritualistic and relaxing, so little of it unexpected that he realizes that all along Cam has been doing it too, lying still for him the way he likes, with a pillow on her face, taking as always just enough air to guarantee that she will lie still for him again the next day, her body a remarkable glory of bone and limp joints; he amazes himself with the simplicity of his luck, to have found his naked body, his naked doll, his quiet evening, and he thanks God the way the long-content do, in a moment of mildly heightened perception prompted by a yawn or an odor. And as usual, Cam gets up from the bed only after he's sated, washes herself, lays out her school clothes, and gets back in bed beside him, positioning her naked bottom so that should he need it in his half-sleep, it's there.

∼

I spent my study halls in the band room, and one morning when I was sitting alone reading over a letter I'd written to Dana in case I ever got her address, Mr. Dombrowski sat down next to me and said,

"Dana's dead." He told me Dana had been shot through a closed door. There were no suspects, not even Andy.

Mr. Dombrowski handed me two brief newspaper clippings, brief because the murder happened out of town, in Philadelphia, where many murders happen, where I had been to a museum and a zoo, and where I had never had a husband, or an apartment, or a violent fight, a threat to my life, a wound of any kind. At the zoo, none of the animals had fought, but slept. I had ridden in a cab with my parents. My mother sat in the middle. My father used to work in Philadelphia, and he was telling us, "That's the corner where I bought hot dogs from a vendor, and that's where I tried to cash a check..." My mother turned and looked at me as though I were her age, and said, "Who cares?" or maybe she said, "Ubi sunt," or "It's hot," or something conspiratory. She hooked her hand behind my knee to keep me from flying out of the cab should there be an accident, and she squeezed firmly, in case I preferred my father's stories to her silence. When we got out, the cab driver asked the name of her perfume.

Mr. Dombrowski said that the same year his mother died he lost two friends in a car accident. They were a married couple, and he was godfather to their child. While he described the wreckage, I folded the clippings inside my letter to Dana, slid the letter back in its envelope, and pulled out the blue felt lining of my flute case and put the envelope underneath, knowing that under these circumstances, Mr. Dombrowski wouldn't yell at me for ruining the case. I kept several things in there that proved I was alive—sheet music Mr. Dheil had given me that was still too hard for me; a note Timmy had passed me in the cafeteria, the only time he had ever acknowledged me during school; report cards that carried particularly flattering comments from teachers; and a certificate for outstanding academic achievement at my old school.

I felt impatient and sad as Mr. Dombrowski groped for some subject, some detail, that would comfort me, or, the longer he talked, for some tidbit that would spring my trap, set off a release in me, a cathartic gust of tears. I waited, listening to him fumble, almost smiling as I thought of saying "Cold...colder...freezing now..." to guide his search for the right words. Dana's death, I was telling myself, could not bother me just then, and what I really needed was someone to say to me, "You're in a bad way, aren't you? Need a break from sex, huh?" and then to give me a ticket for a space capsule ride by myself, centuries long, with nothing more than food, my flute, sheet music, and a stand.

In a pause, we both waited for words, and I felt tears smart in my eyes, realizing he wasn't going to say, "In a bad way, huh?" and then he said, "We can talk about something else," meaning weather or rehearsal or his son's violin lessons. Disappointment caught me the way some waves do at low tide, small, but with unexpected momentum, catching you behind the knees and staggering you, and when he asked me what happened to All-State auditions, his words steadied me, lifted me above the tide to the crisp mundane. I told him I'd been caught up in other things, especially since Aunt Marge had left, and he leaned conversationally over the back of the chair and told me all about the auditions, who had gone, how they did. He even told me about a couple of the poorer players who foolishly dared to try out and embarrassed themselves, confiding in me about my peers in a way that made me uncomfortable, yet he said nothing I couldn't have guessed on my own. Vaguely, pleasantly, I saw the next three years in that band, in that school, stretch out before me. He never suggested I'd made a mistake in not competing for All-State, and even said that considering all the recent upheavals in my personal life, now was not the time to take on the responsibility of membership in another band, implying matter-of-factly that I would have gotten in.

He said he'd been praying for me all along, and suddenly I felt an almost tangible snag of irritation, as though my pant leg caught in a prickle bush. I had been about to tell him about Uncle Scofield, and how we were getting so close and dependent on each other, setting aside pride and differences for the sake of body-sharing, although I was always disgusted with his gruff, ugly clumsiness, and he impatient with my age, falling in love as he said he did with someone too young to operate a motor vehicle. But I stopped myself from telling Mr. Dombrowski because I saw that he couldn't understand, not being a body-sharer himself, and even if he were, to tell him might have been to invite him, and I sensed that I should be exclusive to Uncle Scofield since he needed that security after losing Aunt Marge to another man. Uncle Scofield would be shocked about Dana and would comfort me, and I could lose myself in his grip and pull. I had an abrupt desire to masturbate, so strong my muscles tensed and flushed hot, and I had difficulty breathing.

Mr. Dombrowski asked me, in all tenderness, if I wanted to go to the lavatory, seeming to assume I was upset, so I hid my face, wiped my dry eyes, and felt my soul sink back into the comfort of cold, felt my secret life loom as powerfully as it once did when I was hiding my relationship with Mr. Dheil; I could lie about anything, hide anything, do as I pleased, separated as I was from every other human. If Mr. Dombrowski weren't slumping hatefully, ineffectually in his chair with a satisfied uneasiness, as though his kindness had precipitated my pending catharsis, I could have rocked myself inconspicuously on the edge of the chair the way I did during class or rehearsal when I needed to. I took his advice and went to the girls' room, where I found myself swollen, impossible to touch. I tried to pee, I tried squeezing my thighs together, I looked around for anything to shove inside me. My skin everywhere felt hollow, as though it needed to be pressed closed by Uncle Scofield's weight. I shoved my fist against myself, just to relieve the pressure, and sat on the toilet, feeling perhaps for the first time that I was sick, sin-sick as Grandmom used to say, when the mind and body can no longer be sated and evil has won. "Hell," she said, "is dissatisfaction, misguided desperation, confusion, and eventually, self-destruction." I knew I needed someone to help me relieve myself, and therefore I hated myself the way hospital patients must hate themselves when the nurse lifts their buttocks over a bedpan. The only male at school who could help me was Mark, and I tried to plot a meeting for that day, but it would take too much time and there were too many variables. I decided, though, that I would have Mark, or someone, as my school boyfriend. Such a betrayal of Uncle Scofield would destroy him, and therefore me. I tried to think of an explanation for him—"You know how it is when you've got to have it: I have needs too"—but all I saw was his anger and pain, the kind I had glimpses of during his threats. He threatened me with dog bites and time in the juvenile home if I were to cheat or tell, something Mr. Dheil never did. Mr. Dheil trusted and respected me, we had an implicit—a gentlemen's—understanding. I realized, sitting swollen on the girls' room toilet, that Uncle Scofield had chosen a bright brown painting of a German shepherd's face to hang over his green-flowered velour couch, and I would never forgive him. I could not love him. I would never tell him about Dana. I breathed more slowly and was able to touch myself. I had stinging and burning and itching on and off throughout the days and nights, so the touch of my finger promised to relieve me many ways. I would telephone Mark, and we could talk about Dana. I was capable of cheating on Uncle Scofield. Maybe I had to, physiologically. Dana could have explained it.

I saw Dana on the floor, white without clothing, a round, blood-crusted welt in her chest. I saw her on the floor in my bedroom, her skull bones protruding and her hair matted to the rug. I closed my eyes and began to pant and hold my breath at the same time because a presence arched over me, took me by the ribs in cold, mammoth hands, and I struggled to recognize it, more real than a memory of Uncle Scofield or Mr. Dheil, with the reality of a sibling-ghost, my brother Michael who never lived, as though he had come upon me in the girls' room and now he was all grown up, seven feet tall and angry. I thought, he's going to rape me.

Alone and sweating cold, I was ashamed that I was helpless against my own body. Weak and wretched, I left myself open to invasions by evil spirits. I realized that many times I had masturbated for myself, for Dana and many men, and had never felt any bodily violence. This was the evil that had killed Dana, come upon me now, a force not from within me but from the sphere of souls, where my mother and my grandmother moved safely, but where Dana, and soon I, would be tormented.

Dana had been murdered. Dana had been murdered, far away, and had not told me. Murder was different from a car wreck, or a heart attack, or the slow, almost delicious disease that took my mother. Murder was an evil I had never considered; it had never touched me, and although suicide was something I had thought about, Dana's death had such an invasive force, I was nearly immobile with fear. I made my way back to the band room, and everywhere was Dana's absence, but her absence merely represented Dana, or nothing any-more, since she had been out of town over a month, and had never really been around school much anyway. No one else noticed that her murder filled the corridors like a snake, its fluid ribs bunching and extending. Few people liked Dana. Mr. Dombrowski hated her, but he had taken it upon himself to tell me about her death, letting me know between every kind word that he thought she had been bad for me. Dana wasn't bad for me. Dana's murder was bad for me.

～

Scofield lies awake, controlling his breath, for this is his first night in Cam's bed. Curled beside him, her skinny back spans from his chest to his navel, and her rough heels scrape his knees. Afraid now to touch her at all, he restrains his breathing so his chest doesn't rock against her, and he avoids marveling at this new gaunt form beside him, at the impossible banquet she made of her bones, because when he remembers what she has just offered him, she who openly hates him, who together with Dana rated him a "No Way," he can barely hold back from pounding her again. She lies still and stiffly, for all the world asleep except for her breathing, agitated but regular, and he lies well controlled there, until he begins to sweat from the heavy blankets and her body too close in the narrow bed. He refuses to move, the moment too miraculous, the next day unthinkable, and he believes he'll kill her if she shifts even an inch of blanket off her shoulder, but then the past floods by like fan mail with memories of life's gifts—a birthday party his friends threw for him in high school, a real party, with two kegs of beer and his first girlie movies; the first time a girl he liked said, "I love you"; his first K-9 partner, Adal; the Christmas he received eighty cards; the night he was hospitalized and so many visitors came at once that they had to wait in line; the time Marge said she admired him because he so deeply appreciated sex, and he proposed marriage then because she was the first person to see him for the man he wanted to be. He cries gratefully into Cam's spine, the silent, swelling kind of crying which must feel like the bends, a change in body pressure forcing nitrogen into the blood, distending the veins of the neck and sinuses, a soundless welling of the most deep and unreachable agony. The heat from his suffering soaks his skin, and when he can see that Cam is sweating too, he throws off the covers, gets out of bed, and leaves her there naked, uncovered.

In the dark, he wanders the house unfatigued, negotiating the furniture and doorways blindly, blocking his face with one arm, his body with the other, and sliding his feet. His wet skin, exposed to the cool pneumatics of the house, does not dry. The wind blows over the house, spattering gainless wet snowflakes, and he can hear it clearly, see in his mind's eye how the house crouches helplessly like a hibernating woodchuck unearthed, and the wind streams over it seamlessly in oceans of navy blue gas, an insidious current, rapid on a planet too brittle for such speed. Absently, he sits on the floor in a room, and he senses that outside a woman crosses the yard; her dress and her hair whip, but she does not stagger, and Scofield thinks she would make better progress if she crawled, and he sees the kennels, empty of dogs; the woman is not Cam's mother, who wore, when

Scofield last saw her, bell-bottoms and beads. The woman is not wearing a long, gauzy nightgown, which would make her appear more recognizably ephemeral, but a dark blue fitted dress, too elderly for her young body, and Scofield, frightened that he will recognize her, lies on his back spread-eagled and concentrates on how tiny the house is around him, how great the wind that shifts the house, edges it along the ground; God hates him. A door opens upstairs, and a small voice shouts, "I'm going to tell!" His hands flex as though searching for a grip, but he's weighted down; the wind has seeped in, the pressure in the house is so enormous that, even if the air were innocuous, his lungs could not expand to take it in, and the house tilts as Barghest lifts it in his teeth.

Scofield is in his own bed, wakened just before he thought his alarm was due to go off, and yet it was not set. Cam has beaten him to the shower. Marge is still gone. He sits on the edge of the bed in his robe, and he hopes so fiercely that he didn't do what he may have done that none of the details come to him. All that he can call to mind is an immediacy—he wants to take his shower—and in that is elation and some room for planning—plow the drive if snow accumulated, break ice in the water bowls, sweep out the kennels, run trails mid-morning. At breakfast, Cam sits in the living room fully dressed for school, her shoes on and her books beside her, eating a Pop Tart and watching a cartoon. In the kitchen, he listens to the news on the radio, drinks a cup of instant coffee, and eats two bowls of cornflakes. When Sweeney comes in the back door, the elation ebbs, and he's no longer conscious of the immediate because he's worked with Sweeney every day for seven years and now together they're deciding not to plow the drive because the thin paste of snow will melt. Now they are doing and living what always comes, the early winter morning routine, preparing for the retraining class on trail, and they work more perfectly because their paths are not crossed by Marge, there are no puppies, no pooch perfumes, no nasty glances as she's asked to give up the obedience ring. By ten a.m., the sun is out and the mens' coats are off and the dogs pant jets of steam.

≈

I walked down the crowded hallway carrying the books I took home and brought back again unopened, carrying them against my chest fat with loneliness; the other faces passed me blankly, some familiar, most strange, I could look right at them passing me, all of them thinking: this is the expert on Dana; and I lowered my eyes so they wouldn't ask me: so what happened to Dana? with the implication that she and I weren't really lovers but we were perverted, did things with boys mostly, did drugs, probably masturbated with hairbrushes. I lowered my eyes because I didn't know anything about Dana and never did, my best friend and a liar, who couldn't help lying, didn't really lie since she herself didn't know why she was taken with some people and then just as suddenly others. She didn't know from where her big plans stemmed, her plan for all of us to buy a house together, to join the police academy, to bleach her hair, become a model, give birth to her next baby, start a movement linking animal rights and feminism, stop drinking, start wearing anklets. She herself never knew what her motivation was, never taking the time to search for a theme in herself, a recurrence or a constant, but to me she was as exciting as a horse, she galloped, she spun, she nipped and stomped, she was a male horse, restless on a windy day, fast and exceedingly stupid.

All of her efforts came to some kind of foreseeable failure—if I lined them all up, each matched a crumbling of venture or self-esteem, *Dana, my friend, I never spoke to you about you.* She could listen to me talk about myself because those were stories, and she collected stories, like the one about a man she dated who stole a store's front window, a huge sheet of glass, just because he saw he could, or the one about her next-door neighbor who threw her baby brother out a window because he had a bee up his shirt. To me Dana was wise, knowing all the things she did, the only one who knew when to laugh and laughed out loud all alone, believing that what people thought about her was inconsequential and frighteningly temporary, like herself. So I could not be an expert on Dana, but people asked me at my locker: Dana ran off with Tony's brother? and that was what I had heard, the way they heard it, and it was all I knew, the way they knew it, and quickly it irritated me, because my feelings had opened all around Dana, feelings that hadn't opened even around Mr. Dheil, feelings that never petaled around my mother, but they all bloomed and tilted toward Dana, a neurohormonal response to the steady company of another human, one of the same sex close to my age, experience, body type, one who involved herself with me physically, releasing in me the hormones of orgasm that excite the instincts toward dependency, vulnerability, and devotion, as proven in studies on female baboons. I remembered, as the other band members one by one came up over the course of weeks to ask me about her death, that I originally didn't want to be associated with her, since she disgusted and embarrassed me before I even knew her name—she openly mocked me, calling me "shit nose" because of my friendship with Mr. Dombrowski, pointing out to boys as I passed that I had cute tits, too bad they were in Dombrowski's mitts, coming to school some days as she did looking clean and pretty, lively, young, and smart. I sometimes hated her, ashamed of her dim-witted, near-sighted energy; she seemed so unaware of how plans and decisions were never to be made impetuously; she was unable to deliberate, pouncing into everything except adulthood. Dana snapped at me for being passive, a wet blanket, scolding me by saying this was why I never *did* anything, never went anywhere, always just let things *happen* to me, this was why I got hurt—she said I asked for sex in the way I walked and talked, in the way I tilted my head and lowered my eyes, the way I stood close and smiled, especially by the things I said, so ready to see sex in any context, my legs already parted. She said I asked not just for sex but for a particular kind, the Dheil kind, maybe because Mr. Dheil was the one who taught me how to get along with people. Had she known, she would have accused me of seducing Uncle Scofield, which I wouldn't have had to do if she hadn't left me. If only it were possible that Dana had left some germ of herself in me the way Mr. Dheil did, or the way I had thought Timmy did, one cell of loaded possibility that would shoot like a spider a lasso heavenward to haul down a spirit for me to cultivate and call my own, a body for me to keep in my body for a time, like one of those wooden kachina dolls that holds dolls within dolls, only this time not to empty myself before the separate body within me could live on its own, no longer just a dream born of my confusion and regret but an actual person that Dana and I created without intention or understanding, leaving me to look at this new creature, to say to it, *how are you possible?*

During class the lectures, like homilies, passed strangely in and out of my hearing now that Dana was dead and touched me only through reprimand by implication, reminding me that I was falling behind, or rather, something had pushed me, causing me to fall, and I had trouble talking to people, the way I did when I first arrived at the school, because other people lived differently from me, immediately in the globes of their eyes, while I saw myself as someone who lived yards and yards behind my eyes, as in a large, dark room with two almond-shaped windows. The only time I lived up against that pellucid gel was when Dana was around, Dana, who shoved me right up to my eyes so that I lived immediately, saw all around myself, and couldn't pay attention to my dark internal drone, so that I forgot myself and played.

≈

Scofield crouches in the brush behind a large twist of briars. The day is dark and unseasonably warm, yet with no threat of rain, and therefore unlike any he can remember. When the wind shifts, he can hear the crack and squish of his pursuers' footsteps, the dog bounding after each of the dead-end traps he left, then quickly, and with more determination, setting to the trail again while the man restrains and balances. Somehow, squatting in the earth as it thaws at such a wrong time, thaws without bugs and sprouts, on a day that reminds him of no other day, Scofield cannot shake the recognition of what Cam's body has become for him, a feeding place, like a breast to a baby, or a syringe that injects nutrients into him, and while he ingests its fluids he's aware at once of a dependency and a power, a self-degradation and self-exaltation. He has gotten rough with her. He recalls remorsefully that the night before he stripped her in front of the TV, bent her between his legs as he sat on the couch, and held her for over an hour, sometimes just sitting without moving, just watching his shows, with her body propped between his legs, savagely limp.

He doesn't come as often anymore, and it doesn't matter. With Marge and others, sex was always climax directed, the quality of it dependent on the speed and intensity of orgasm, but with his sister, and now with Cam, sex is a journey to a place in his brain; he sometimes pictures it, a black passageway so close he has to force himself through its sopping sponginess, the air damp and unbreathably rank with the stench of her vagina, raw as it is with infection, and as he nears the back of his mind, the passageway dips downward, toward the base of his skull, and there he rests in a silent pocket of pitch-black liquid, where only the riveting sound of his own heartbeat and the images of atrocities reach him; the images play on the surface of the liquid, flash and ripple over his wet skin, her body facedown on the bed, hanging twisted in a window drape, her severed head with eyes blank and mouth slack, and she does not cough or gag—his heart and the images are the two things that keep him alive; nothing, nothing keeps him alive like his dead doll. His main fear when he isn't in his brain place is that he will emerge from that place and find he has killed her, which means she will soon rot and fall away and he won't be able to go back, it will all be over.

He crouches in the bushes at the base of a slope, under gray-padded skies, under branches like veins brittle with dried blood, the earth underneath him steaming, all waste and untimely festering. He is a man he would shoot. He is a man he would throw in jail and leave to ridicule, bruisings, stabbings, and rapes; in the community of a prison, he would be leprously low. He rises and runs farther into the woods, veering off, then backtracking, heading in a scrambled way toward a brook. He catches scraps of Harding's exclamations: the lead is tangled, the trail longer than Scofield promised, the weather fucking hot. Scofield falls on his knees in the brook and pauses there, arms and legs and face washed in the cold. By the sudden directness of the pursuit, Scofield can tell that the cop has stopped tracking by scent alone and is following the footsteps in the muck. He lifts his face and shouts, "You should be *scent* training!" and the reply floats back, "Fuck you," and Scofield rises and runs back toward the house in a wide arc; the dog's distant wheezing is the huff of a dog pack, the heavy foot thumps are the muddy, calloused feet of Wild Julia; his wet clothes resist him, his chest begins to fail, Julia is naked and fast, her dogs—his old dogs—lower, stretch, lean their bodies into full gallop, and he tells himself there is no pack of wild dogs, there is no wild girl, Julia.

~

We walked through the woods carrying six-packs in the dark, and I wanted to think about how to act with these guys now that Dana was gone and as a freshman I had little justification to be with them, but all I could think about was how weird the weather was for February—the wind and the temperature were mild, and mushrooms and fungi and mosses thrived, and strange birds, even in the winter dark, twittered invisible in the bare branches. "This weather is so weird," I said, but no one answered. In a small clearing inappropriate for camp fires, we made a damp little fire and sat on logs or on once-purposeful heavy fabrics, such as discarded bedspreads, or just on the ground. There were two other girls, both taken, six boys, and Mark and I. Tread and Mark evidently weren't friends anymore, Mark having "graduated" permanently to this group. Once we were settled, everybody wanted to know about Dana, and Mark and I and a couple others who knew her got to talk about her, remembering stories. The others had better stories than mine, many I hadn't heard before, but everyone knew I was her closest and most recent friend, and I could sit comfortably on all the stories as if I knew them, so powerful was her sway that it buoyed me above everyone. Someone had a bottle of grain, and someone else, maybe Mark, had Quaaludes, and the two girls just stuck to the Quaaludes because they were trying to lose weight. They talked on about Dana, which frightened me because we all knew she had been murdered, and nothing could be said about her that didn't rush straight and unspoken to that black hole. Something sad shook all the trees, and Mark took my hand, so I must have sighed and shaken the trees and Mark's hand around mine must have been very significant, but I was looking into the black woods, thinking, "I'm looking into the woods all sad, and Mark is holding my hand—we're lovers." Everyone fell silent, respectful of my sadness, and one girl said, "Isn't it terrible?"

I could tell this group wouldn't become an orgy, especially on the wet ground, but after some time a pipe came around, and came around again, and the grain, and the 'lude, and the beer, like fresh water after the scorch of the pipe, made a whirlpool in my chest so that I was very heavy on the ground, sucked down into it. The girls, after staggering off with me for a pee, joined their boyfriends a shadowy distance from the fire; some of the other guys left, and some stayed sitting on the log and talked like men at a bar. Mark and I stayed close to the fire. Mark was saying that Dana's death really made him think about his own death, how it could come any time, and he should make something of himself soon, and I said I should just devote myself to music and say fuck off to everything and everyone else. Mark said he couldn't think of what he should devote himself to, and he considered marrying me, then confessed that he had loved Dana and started to cry. Before I knew it, I was curled up on the ground crying loudly, saying how lonely I was and nobody liked me and I was too young for all of them, they'd forget me tomorrow, and I could never be a famous flutist or have a nice husband and babies because I was a slut and I was screwing my uncle, he made me pretend I was a corpse every night and this was the first night I got away from him and I didn't want to die, I was afraid to die, I was so scared to die, so scared someone was on his way to shoot us all right there in the woods. The guys on the log fell silent, and I pulled myself together enough to realize I was embarrassed and that Mark was plotting to have a gang beat the shit out of my uncle. I didn't have to worry, the guys said, that man would never touch me again. I'd done the right thing by telling them. They asked me some questions about just what my uncle did to me and how often, but the cry made me tired and spinning-sick. I laid my head in Mark's lap, he stroked my hair, and he and the guys told stories about perverts. Something very small and alive moved under a bush, and a breeze rasped in the branches, and I was cold, and a sky empty of souls and evil spirits arced high, high above all of us, and I was rising there, soaring in peace. Tomorrow the guys would have just one more pervert story to tell—the sight of my face in the hallways at school would set them to telling my story in homeroom and study hall. Mark would try to be my boyfriend, and I would go back to Uncle Scofield, remembering the feel of the empty sky that I'd had.

Mark helped me when I got sick and said he was going to take me to his house because I couldn't go home to my uncle. I saw myself half-sleeping in a car, alone, parked on a neighborhood street, then Mark's parents in their robes and messy hair helping me inside a brightly lit house with carpeting and new wallpaper into a guest room and a bed deep with clean blankets. I imagined I was sick again and I fell asleep in one of his mother's nightgowns, and in my dream the back of that nightgown was split and tied like a hospital gown, and I was anesthetized on a stretcher and people were running with me.

"I can't go home with you," I said. If Mark and his parents helped me and ruined Uncle Scofield and fixed me all up to be returned to my father, my body would still be shuffled by others' bodies—I would not be in control—when all I wanted was to be free of bodies, free to study, to play music. Dana had controlled others' bodies; she said, "Go to this party," or "Get out of my car," and they did. Mr. Dheil could have left me alone in my clothes, left my mind dry and free to whirl up from the ground like dust instead of tamping it with his sex, which distracted me from everything else. Even then, while it was happening with him, I hated him for that, knowing he could have blown into my ears gold music dust instead of his heady, deadening steam and that his affection was a lie because it didn't stay with me, keeping me strong. At his house, he convinced me I was an exceptionally erotic being, but the rest of the week I crept about, a star-nosed mole driven from its narrow hole. When I sniffled that I was unworthy of anyone's attention, he went into the kitchen and came back with a fresh, cold plum. "You are like this," he said, and handed it to me. "You're a satisfying, newly plucked fruit. Bite it." I did. "That's how you taste to me," he said.

Mark's parents would tell me what I was to them, a nice girl gone astray, ruined by accident, by others' influence, the way Mr. Dombrowski seemed to think I was. I could not go home with Mark, nor could I go home to be Uncle Scofield's rubber doll, not after seeing Mark and his friends disgusted with my story, reawakening an uneasiness I'd had that if it was wrong for little children to share bodies, and wrong for most other girls, perhaps it was wrong for me too. Just what was wrong with it baffled me, but I decided then, in trying to explain to Mark why I wouldn't go home with him, that sex with my uncle was wrong because it took away my freedom to be like everyone else my age, even though Scofield and I weren't really related and his wife was divorcing him. Mark and the others, who were beginning to listen to us, agreed. In fact, everyone seemed to respect me not only for my decisiveness, but because I had slept with Scofield in the first place. In private, I had always believed that joining my body to an adult's aged me not only because an adult wanted me and trusted me to satisfy and to keep quiet, but also because sliding my cells along older cells gave me a physical kind of wisdom—maturity in youth. This privilege I sensed, but I could not depend upon it since it was fleeting and it separated me from everyone else by precipitation—I settled siltlike at the bottom of the school community without anyone but me knowing why—and if it weren't for music I was really nothing more than skin, a fleshy creature my mother bore with regret. Mark and his friends were looking me in the face as I spoke now, and, glancing over my body, they seemed to be deciding with attempted sobriety that if an adult male could want me I was an unusual and probably talented catch. I kept my final decision to myself: I would take away Scofield's freedom, stifle his dreams, control and frighten him; I would go home and rape *him*.

∼

Cam is out for the evening, and Scofield sits in his office, working at his desk. He tries not to turn around to look at the doorway. The day was so warm that he threw windows open, and he has not gotten around to shutting them, so that in the dark, cold air sifts like invisible sand over the window sills, heaping and hissing on the floors. It laps in waves, burying his feet, but it could be Barghest, crawling under his desk the way old Master did, to sleep on his shoes like a pile of laundry. He listens for Cam to come home. On the edge of his hearing, a flute sounds, a barely audible, halting melody, the overture she has played daily since she first moved in. Perhaps Cam has not gone out with friends at all, but lied to him so as to spend the evening in peace. Maybe she's with some boy who'll climb into the window at night and slit his throat. She could be at the police station. The last thought makes him laugh—none of the guys would believe her.

He has dreamed for so long about winning her affection, but her silent compliance is beginning to jade him—she is a witch, a psychic, a medium. If he says to a dog, "Stay," and it stays, it does so by decision, weighing in every successive second the consequences of breaking a *stay*, struggling with its own conflicting interests, but Cam, when he says, "Now," and begins to make love to her, disappears, almost in a kind of out-of-body travel. Leaving her body behind for him to enjoy is exactly the kind of pleasure he wishes her to give, but he's begun to worry about where her mind goes. He imagines she's in her room waiting for him in one of her death trances and her mind walks the house in the form of a large, black-pelted dog. Out of body, her mind takes the form of a young girl, a girl with thick calves and upper arms, with hair like a mooring cable down her back.

Scofield gets up and looks out the front window. He wishes he'd given her a curfew—when she asked if she could go out he was busy with some stupid cop who used a choke like a fairy and his dog was froggy all over him and Scofield was about to tell the guy to just quit K-9 and give the dog to a *man*, when here comes Cam in her woolly-lined denim jacket, looking like any other kid saying, "Hey Unc, can I go to my friend's party for a couple of hours tonight?" In front of the faggot, what was Scofield to say, with the dog chopping its own spit at Cam and her smiling. "Nice dog," she says to the cop, his neck sweating and his arm about to bust the seam of his shirt; the dog's pulling so hard, something has to give, so Scofield says, "Yeah, all right, get the hell away from here," but next time he's going to say "No, we'll talk about it later," real fatherly.

He knows nothing about her friends. Nothing about her. He can't even remember where she came from—he tries, but he can't remember her first day with them. He recalls little pictures of her, strolling along the fence with Timmy, asleep on the couch covered with music, giving a friendly pat to the idiot Harry's back, talking familiarly with old Sweeney, who winks at her, glaring at Marge, glaring at him, giggling with Dana, sitting in Dana's car out front for hours, watching old movies in the dark with Dana, looking him right in the face and saying she only smells like smoke because Dana was smoking. And in all those full-color flashes of Cam come full-color flashes of Wild Julia bloodied in a cabin. He sits down on the couch, and he can see Julia in his house—selling candy bars for a girls' club, bringing her dog to him because it barks too much. He remembers for the first time that he has met her before—or he imagines he met her before. The difference seems so slight to him that he wonders if his vision of her rape and murder in a cabin might have been something he participated in, even to the point of burying her on his property, under the foundation of one of the kennels.

Suddenly, there's an oppressive odor to the house, and he runs to the kitchen and sniffs at all the refrigerator shelves, at the garbage can. He hollers "Barghest!" because if it doesn't appear it may never have appeared, in which case Julia is not buried under the end kennel. He calls it again, and his own dogs reply in comforting chorus, and he leans on the counter realizing he never taught Barghest its name. Twice he tries to track it, following its path from the kitchen through the living room and up the stairs. Perhaps, as the priest explained on the phone, the dog will only appear when Cam is in the house. He tries to remember if he's ever seen it without Cam in the house, but he recalls nothing. He checks her room to see if she's in, believing he may have gotten the date of her party wrong, and in her room, he cannot remember ever being in her bed with her; in fact, he's at a loss as to what Cam looks like at all.

~

There are many channels between the living—sebaceous glands, enzymes, eardrums, ocular nerves—through which we communicate incomprehensible complexities. The eardrum was my favorite, a crisp little disk, a tiny diaphragm blocking physical impurities. Although many sounds enter the ear that cause nonphysical impurities to embed and root in the soul, the ear canal is the way music enters—while the monstrosity of music swells off the stage to scratch its spine along the auditorium ceiling and walls, it divides into hundreds of micromonsters that pad down hundreds of pairs of furry, waxy hallways, only millimeters wide. Eyes may be souls' windows, but the hearing ear is the door, always open. People who were revived from comas claimed they'd heard everything all along. If Uncle Scofield had said to me again, "Lie still," I would have refused, too frightened and tired of our quiet act, a funeral parlor play in which I had what I thought was the easy part, the corpse, lying about while he arranged me in taxidermic poses, bit, petted, and wept on my skin, then made his quick injection, and I held my breath and waited for his fluids to run their stinging course like Novocaine, formaldehyde, curing me, oxydizing my skull. I would have refused and said, "Let's be different tonight," because he had no variety, only the repetitive requirements—I lay still, he climbed about—during which I rehearsed the All-State audition music in my mind, even though the audition had closed. At first I tried to let the death-act bring me close to my mother, sometimes imagining I was her, dead in her bed; I saw the blankets my father had pushed aside, I saw her limbs grooved and rippled as a runner's yet sapped and shriveled by illness, I saw how her back and the backs of her thighs were one long bruise. One time, as I imagined I was her and played the corpse, I saw from above how Uncle Scofield leaned over the body, saw how he deferred to it while defiling it, saw how helpless it was, and I realized for the first time how alone I was, naked and dead without any possibility of redeeming myself, gone and alone, never achieving my mother's embrace, my breath stifled and never living in my flute again, my eardrums rattling, doors on an empty house, my soul drowned in silence. From then on when he was with me, I occupied my brain instead with music, which was to me a reed trafficking air to one immersed in a swamp, an IV keeping a patient alive while the sternum is split and the chest cavity cranked open. Mark and his friends thought sex with Scofield should stop— easy for them to say; easy for me to agree, but the only way it could stop was for Uncle Scofield to say one more time, "Lie still," and for me to refuse and to take over, to have *him* lie still, a dead animal drying in the sun on an open road, and to invade him with the handle of a spatula—to stick it down his throat and hiss like him, "Don't choke, holdyourbreath, holdit!"

Instead he said, "Take your bath."

He led me firmly by the arm upstairs and ran the bathwater. The bathroom walls drizzled with steam, and the air in the room was yellow with haze and the light from grimy bulbs. "The water's too hot," I said. "I already had a shower today." Uncle Scofield undressed and lowered himself in the water. His skin turned red, and he sighed there, massaging his penis with his eyes closed, his legs looking, in the rocking water, impossibly angled and waving. "Be a good niece," he said. "Undress and get in." If he had just said his usual, "Stop tensing up," I could have come in on two, playing "Golden Jubilee," but instead I was standing, sweating, watching him massage himself and relax against the porcelain, his chins sagging into his neck. He was a preacher, a mayor, a great ape taking a moment from his power to loll in weakness. "No," I said, remembering what the boys in the woods had said. "This is perverted."

He opened one eye and raised his eyebrows. He was smiling. "Get in," he said, his voice muted and sluggish, stuffed with steam. I stood for a moment longer, my clothes already wet, and I began to undress because he had already shoved me once that evening for defying him, but then, seeing that he had stopped moving and slumped as though sleeping, I turned for the door.

∾

Nine dogs are chained ten feet apart to the fence. They've been there for days, furious, barking all day and howling through the night. Scofield hasn't been able to get people to stay away, least of all Sweeney, so he's fired him and canceled all the classes and unplugged the phone to shut off the flack.

Whenever he wakes up, day or night, he feeds and waters all the dogs, not wanting them to go without because he's forgotten them. Their shit and piss have begun to overwhelm the kennel, but there's something natural in that—the place smells the way those farms on the highway do, those with big, low barns and no animals in sight.

Cam crawls up the stairs on all fours and says, "God, I need a bath." She runs the water so loudly he can hear it wherever he is on the grounds, and she calls him. "I can't do it myself," she says, an impatient child, and she plays her flute while the water runs, but when he gets to the bathroom, she's gone. The water is cold because he ran it himself hours ago. It's so hard to keep it hot for her. He drains the tub and runs the water scalding hot; that way maybe it'll be just right for her when she gets home.

The last time she was home, she came in the door in the middle of the night, stinking of booze and wood smoke, and went right to sleep. She woke around noon, was sick, and went back to bed. He heard her later in the kitchen, shouting, "Goddamn it. There's no food." She slept on the couch while he got groceries and made dinner, and after she ate, smiling boldly at him, he asked her who the hell she thought she was, staying out late like a drunken slut, and when she smiled again, he jumped up in a rage and grabbed at her jeans, "I'll rip these off you and suck the fucker right out of you." But she just giggled like a whore and took the shoving and bruises and leaned her breasts on his head as he sniffed at her.

"You won't find anything there," she said, and for the first time her soul was right in her eyes looking directly at him, the languid, confident gaze of a Newfoundland, amused at his terror and confusion, like Barghest. "I want you," she said, drawing some kind of power from an unseen, unfathomable source, and he let her go, trying to grasp all the possible connotations of her words.

"You are evil," he said, and without another thought he struck her with both hands, a blunt shove meant to drive that spirit out of his little girl, but instead she fell off the chair and lay coughing up her dinner onto the floor in a slow heap, eyes and nose red and wet. Her gagging was a design on his sympathy. He remembered the four-year-old standing in a bathtub, choking with a feigned reprimand in her eyes. The last time Camille was in his house, Scofield dragged her up the stairs and ran a bath.

It's hard to tell how long she's been gone because he hears her talking on the phone to Julia in the middle of the night and then Cam and Julia take a bath together, naughty girls, and lock the door.

～

I pictured my mother and Dana together. They sat at the kitchen table in my mom's house, near the cockatiel cage. The bird made small, dusty noises, stepping forth and back and forth again, giving his feathers a shake. Occasionally a drop of water from his beak dotted the place mats. Dana had on her boots and favorite brown flannel shirt. She had a fresh, unlit cigarette lying next to her teacup, and she fidgeted with it but had no intention of smoking it. My mother was the way she was when everyone could see she was dying but left it up to my father to talk her into seeing doctors. Her hair hung in thin, lovely blond sheets. She never let the roots come in dark until the last weeks. She and Dana leaned across the table toward each other. I strained to hear what they were saying, but couldn't think of anything for them to say.

My mother wouldn't have liked Dana. She would've let me spend time with her, too tired to protest, to explain, but not too tired to avoid getting into a conversation herself with Dana, the two of them intimate over tea. "Men are essential," Dana said to my mother; "most of the people I have the greatest love and respect for are men." Dana added that she just didn't *believe* in these men. "Look what they do to your daughter."

"We're all daughters," my mother said, "only daughters and sons. None of us has any real responsibility." She said her own mother thought she could take care of everyone and was always frustrated. "We're only parents to ourselves."

I wanted to interrupt, to join them at the table, where I could feel again the familiar rough wood of the chairs, feel the aura of secrecy that was my mother, and inhale her. I wanted, under the table, to press the side of my thigh against hers and to know that what she said was true: she was never, from my birth, responsible for me; she didn't want me—I was terribly, wonderfully free.

Dana said she disagreed completely. She said something about parents teaching children to take care of themselves by assuming authority over them—she was daring, presumptuous with my mother, reveling in adult banter. She said she believed each person was obligated not only to all mankind, but to all creatures, to the planet. Her murder darkened the room.

I could see that my mother, like me, had the greatest respect for Dana's murder. She nodded, granting Dana the point that in some situations, we were obligated to preserve the lives of others. I looked for them, but the baby souls had withdrawn.

Dana went on, saying things that sounded like my grandmother's religious talk, although she was careful to make it understood that she did not believe in God. She quoted 2 Corinthians. She led the discussion and seemed to be winning, her life pulsing in the swing of her knee—she tapped her heels, fluffed her hair, spun the teaspoon between her knuckles. She was impetuosity and generosity.

Yet my mother, in her white robe, sat still in the wisdom of her illness. Beside her, Dana looked foolish. The only truth in what Dana said was happy accident. "At the risk of criticizing," my mother said, "do for yourself what you would have others do for you." My mother drained her surroundings; she was quiet greed, sucking power from all she was offered and never making requests. Her life and mine were forced upon her. She received her death like a change in the weather. Most men assumed by her looks that she was unstable and erotic and stupid, and using that, she became dangerous. I knew these things about her implicitly, from the way a stranger at the dry cleaners treated her to the things my father said. "Your mother's full of shit," he'd say, meaning she was deceptively capable. Seeing Dana and my mother at the kitchen table, I could believe my mother was dead, but I realized that I would never believe Dana was dead. She moved there, across from my mother, fingering the cigarette, sliding it around the saucer, smiling down into her teacup.

~

Scofield puts down the crowbar with a clank and rests himself on one of the sheets of concrete he has pried up from a kennel floor. The weather has stayed strangely warm for this time of year, and occasionally a fly lights on his bare arm to suck at his salt. After cracking and lifting a few more feet of concrete, he can begin digging. Barghest is back, hanging about all the time now, although Scofield rarely sees it. He senses it, and so do the other dogs, seeming to have accepted it as the alpha male and resigned themselves to passive panting in their cells. They lie for hours stretched on their sides, or pace with dull eyes. The dogs chained to the fence continue to complain, yelping and digging and trying to turn on each other. They spill their food and water; they gnaw bloody-gummed at their chains.

Scofield rises and works several more hours, hacking and prying at the concrete. The muscles in his arms and back tremble, and he feels his sweat draining his salt and oils, shrinking his body mass. Night falls abruptly, and he begins his digging. He's been working so steadily that the dogs fall silent, reacting not at all to the scrape of the shovel or the smell of wet dirt.

He does not think about the object of his search, but instead thinks of Cam. He tries to recall when and how she left and whether or not she left, just as he tries to recall when he last slept and whether or not the dogs have been tended to. His frustration no longer makes him break down—he draws strength, determination, from it. It drives his shovel. If he finds nothing after removing the floor of every kennel, then all his fantasies are harmless. If he finds one of Julia's severed limbs, then every thought he's ever had is indistinguishable from his memories; experiences and stories cross, merge, usurp each other, and his imagination has a power independent of his will, creating both the wonder of a well-trained dog and a butchered girl, not just after time has muddled the boundaries of past realities, but immediately. He might have killed Cam.

He looks over the floors of the neighboring four kennels, gutted, and wonders if he should have dug more deeply. The gravel of a skeletal hand may lie within reach of his next shovel chop. Occasionally, he walks through the house and looks for Cam's body. Barghest might have dragged the body into the woods. As soon as this thought passes, he sees it—her naked body slides in mysterious starts and stops across the lawn toward the woods, as though drawn by an uncooperative magnet. And yet, there is no body or Barghest, and Scofield has no memory of Cam's death.

What he remembers mistrustfully is a bath. "Just stand. Or kneel—you're too tall now," he says, motioning her into the water.

She hesitates. "Why?" She's got her hand on the doorknob; she means to leave. "Now I have to act alive?"

That's not what he wants. He struggles to explain, but he's not sure of himself. In his dreams the girl cooperates; her size changes to suit him, he can slide her into his pants, over his cock, and zip up and go out to work the dogs. He can immerse her in the tub and snorkel his way to her ovaries, which he plucks and eats like pomegranates. Yet here she stands, dressed, suspicious, unwilling, threatening to leave, she who until this point played possum cunt for him better than his sister or his sleeping wife. "Do like you did when you were four," he says. "Stand here and let me soap you up."

He's about to add that this time he'd rather she didn't get all righteous and upset again, the way she did as a child, squeaking at him and scolding, but she interrupts him with questions, angered and adult-looking, asking what happened when she was four, as if she had no memory of their first encounter, as if it hadn't haunted her too, as if it had meant no more to her than going to a little neighbor's birthday party to play pin-the-tail-on-the-donkey, only to go to bed that night and sleep the whole insignificant day into oblivion. She turns for the door, and he lurches out of the tub, the water making a roaring noise that frightens them both, sending him surging against her. His nudity making him weak and faltering, he pulls and fumbles at her clothes, recalling for an exciting moment that he struggled to undress the four-year-old too, and she had fought him until she was in the water. Yet no more of it parallels his memory or any of his fantasies, even those that defied and disturbed him. The teenager is too big and suddenly willful. She tries to knee him, she flings a dish of dusty carved and colored soaps at him, she tries to jab him in the face with a toothbrush. She cries, "I don't belong to you," over and over. He pins her arms, and then she's free of him, pulling down the shower curtain in a succession of rips and pops. He tells her he'll tell her father and make her pay for the curtain, and then the flush of desperation on her face startles him. "You're insane," he says to her, and she's upon him, jarring him to the floor, bruising him with her elbows as she forces the curtain around his face. At once he wants to escape her and at the same time enter her. He pulls her to him, burning his shaft against the fabric of her pants. He tries to rock her into submission, abandon, and yet she shoves and stretches at the plastic curtain until for a moment his breath sucks against it, blocked, and he convulses. She's standing and stepping on it, pinning it against his face, and then when he's able to roll over and gasp, she's gone.

~

On the bus, I held Uncle Scofield's wallet on my lap because it was too big to fit into my pockets. The man at the bus station had noticed that and had seen I had no other baggage with me except my flute case. "I've got a minor here," he said to someone I couldn't see, "a little girl."

Another man came and looked me over. "Where you off to?" he said.

They asked if my parents knew I was taking a little trip, and I was so afraid they'd stop me that I told them I had already run away from home and was running back. I had stolen my father's wallet, and now I wanted to go home. They smiled, and one moved toward the phone. "Wait," I said. I told them to call Father Robert, the priest friend of my grandmother, the only person I could think of who had known my family and could help me get back to my father. I gave them the name of the town and the church. I listened while the man phoned

Father Robert and told my story, and I prayed. Then I heard the man tell Father where to meet my bus when it arrived.

After the phone call, I had an hour and a half to wait for the bus, and the men brought me donuts and orange juice. They kept asking me to play my flute for them, to sing for my breakfast, but I didn't. I could tell I didn't have to.

Looking out the bus windows, I noticed that, foggy dawn or not, the journey home looked alarmingly unfamiliar. I tried to relax. I wasn't very tired after walking all night because I had slept, hung over, most of the day before, but I reclined the seat and closed my eyes as if to nap, one hand resting on the wallet, the other on my flute case, and I thought about Dana, how alive she was, how I could call her up in my mind anytime I wanted and she laughed there the way she did, tucking her hair behind one ear and peering slyly up through her bangs. But my mother was dead. Her spirit would never visit me. I had seen my mother dead for all time—her skin arranged on her face, not sagging a bit as it should have since she was on her back. She was heavier, pumped full of something too colorful. Her hair had been dyed, but not the shade she used as her emblem. Her nostrils appeared solid, uniformly black, trick tunnels as in a cartoon.

At the viewing, I kept looking for Mr. Dheil, who said he would show up, but he never came. Except for the body, I was the main focus of the gathering, people fawning in ways that made no sense to me, apologizing for her death and then touching my shoulders. If they had cared for me, they would not have let me see that my mother lay at such a level and location that from everywhere in the room you had to notice she wasn't breathing. The stillness of her chest riveted the eye. It was a stunning centerpiece, a vortex. I wanted to fly at it with fists raised, and yet it was impossible not to stand, stare, and take private inventory—I felt my weight balance itself in the soles of my shoes, the cilia in my sinuses waved in the surf of my breath, my fingertips mercilessly recorded the damp texture of my pockets. As long as I was in the room, from hours before the service until the last stammering well-wisher left, I could see that her round breasts, manifestations of my entrance into the world, did not rise and fall. I had lain in the water-cradle of her body, rocked gently by the involuntary motion of her lungs, a mechanism which had lulled me beyond birth, despite her will or my awareness. The room smelled of flowers and cigarettes, and not at all of patchouli.

At Uncle Scofield's, when I played my flute the dogs Darcy and Ben had gotten up on the bed like two children in pajamas and listened. In that room on the dresser my sheet music sat stacked in a Manila folder—Overture in B Flat, "Cordoba," "Sunflower Slow Drag." The only clothing I had was what I was wearing—I remembered my favorite dark green corduroys were in the hamper, and my Easter dress, a puffy pink cotton shift with a wide, elaborate lace collar, hung in the closet under plastic, worn only once before, a gift from my mother. In the closet too was my jewelry box, white and stenciled with gold hearts, something I had owned as long as I could remember. It held tangled chains, my turquoise ring, freshwater pearl earrings, a crucifix and Saint Christopher medal my grandmother gave me, large, ugly onyx earrings that were my grandmother's, and several rings, bracelets, and necklaces that were my mother's, among them a big diamond ring that, when my mother used to clean it, looked clear enough to drink. On the closet floor I'd left an old collapsible music stand of Mr. Dheil's that no longer folded up the right way. In my desk were my father's letters, brief, but always accompanied by photographs, his apartment, his office, the office building, a duck pond, his car, his girlfriend, the front of the store at which he bought me my Christmas gift, a handmade alpaca wool sweater from Oregon. I still had, in one of the dresser drawers, a T-shirt of Dana's that I'd borrowed at her house one time when we got rained on. It was an old Bicentennial shirt, blue with once-shiny white satin stars sewn across the shoulders, and the number 200 in red-and-white striped fabric stitched across the chest. The stars and digits were coming off at the corners, and the fabric had a loose, soft sheerness to it from being frequently worn and well washed. Although I'd had it several months and it smelled like Aunt Marge's laundry, I couldn't wear it without feeling myself slouch like Dana, laugh and twist my hair around my finger the way Dana did. I tucked my jeans in my boots when I wore the shirt, and I slumped forward whenever I sat down, as though her solid arm was flung about my neck. On my nightstand I'd left a German porcelain figurine Aunt Marge had given to me, called "Girl and Dog." It was a little girl, toddler-shaped with a high forehead and wispy yellow curls. Her dress flounced around her frilly bloomers and dimpled knees. She stood on tiptoe to hug her dog, whose eyes flashed with good humor, intelligence, and protectiveness, and who grinned with his delicate ceramic teeth, one of them pink from a brushstroke meant for the tongue. The breed was some sort of large, sassy terrier, like Ben only all pale gray. The girl's arms and face were partly buried in his coat, her eyes closed. Her curls blended with his.

All would be sent to me.

∾

Scofield gets off the couch, where he sleeps, rising stiffly to go back to his digging. His days are Alaskan, all dark or all light or some blend of both, and randomly short or long. He has nearly emptied the cupboards, eating meals of dry spaghetti or a can of kidney beans. He has never before lived and worked so efficiently, and with pride he sits down to a breakfast of potato flakes and water. Only the dogs upset him, looking at him with eyes of misery, both empathetic and reproachful. The two Cam had spoiled, Ben and Darcy, are the most irritating, crying with disillusionment, Cam gone and their house privileges denied.

He drops his breakfast dishes into the sink full of cold soapy water, where he keeps all his plates, pans, and utensils, and goes out into the dark. The air and sky are deep black, silent, and still, and Scofield makes his way with confident blindness directly to his shovel, bends briskly to retrieve his digging gloves from the ground, puts them on, and hefts the shovel. It occurs to him that he's become the man Marge always wanted—distant, determined, mysterious, completely lacking interest in her. He finds himself strangely distracted from his musings and his work. The quiet and the darkness are too thick. The sound of the shovel echoes off the night, interrupting his rhythm, and the stillness magnifies the ringing of his ears. Occasionally, a dog smacks its lips and squeals in midyawn. The hindrances create a livid tightness in his chest, and he leans harder into each chop of the shovel blade, driving his concentration deeply into the hole. The blade keeps clashing against stone, stopping him short, giving off flashes that are either sparks or tricks of the eye from the jolt. He climbs into the hole to wiggle the stones free, a dentist extracting a giant's teeth.

As he pulls loose one rock, an unusual, papery clod of earth falls from one side. In the dark that paints him with uneasiness, he sits on the edge of the hole and lifts the strange lump of dirt in one gloved hand. He could easily have rigged himself a work light. He wants at once to see clearly, without fussing with hooks and wires. He tips the object in his hand, gently separating it from the dirt and gravel. It feels flimsy, a mesh of roots or a tangle of zippers. As if on cue, an eerie chorus of invisible birds breaks upon his ears. He looks up quickly—if a ray of dawn has cast itself across the sky, it has not yet touched his cell of cement and dirt. The birds' chatter hurries him; he cups the object loosely and shakes it. It seems to break into two sections in his hands, and its sudden fracture startles him, as though in disjunction it snaps with life. Panicked, he tosses the pieces onto the lawn. More piping voices join in the black din, and as the sky reveals the woolly tops of winter trees, black fibers against blue-violet, Scofield stands in the grass looking down, watching the image develop as though in a tray of photographic solution, a flat-faced skull the size of a child's fist, wide ribs, a curved backbone, spindles of limbs.

He waits no longer for the picture to come clear, just long enough for the skeleton's position to register—fetal. Self-recognition collapses on him like a tent—nothing could satisfy him as much as piercing the body cavity of a miniature human, still warm, the slip of gristle, the clamp and friction of ribs, the little heart pulsing. Tiny hands closed on the folds of his finger joints.

Somewhere, somehow, he has tasted this most inviolable delicacy. The experience spans the four horizons of his mind, its colors obliterating the mental doodles of Julia and Cam—Marge's baby, miscarried? aborted? by him?—found in the blood-smeared bathtub, then buried under the kennel. The details fall away, blotted by the brush strokes of red and white porcelain as Scofield crashes through the shed, where he turns on the light and chooses quickly an extra-long prong collar and a thick nylon tracking lead. The birds' music maddens him with its laziness, its drawn-out randomness. In the house, as he runs up the stairs he can't hear it over his footsteps and the sound of Marge's voice as she lies bleeding weakly in the bedroom, repeating "Sweetheart? Call the doctor." He pulls down the folding attic stairs and feels a challenge—he's faster than Barghest, who won't make it up the steps in time for one final jolly-jowled entrance. Scofield throws open the attic window and yanks the collar and lead over his head, the prongs scraping his face and scalp and pinching the tender skin of his neck hard. From the attic window he can see one kennel, regimentally rectangular, tidy, placid, and famil-iar, caging the furry circles of curled up dogs. In dismay he wonders if he's done any digging at all—one glance at his muddy pants tells him only that he *may* have been digging; he can never know. Whether or not he has committed the crimes of his most caustic fantasies, whether or not they have remained safely jeweled in the cushion of his brain, he is a profaner, someone that cops bludgeon to death in the woods. He turns to look once behind him, and the face of Barghest does not brim the lip of the attic stairwell. He attaches the lead to the prong collar, ties the other end to a roof beam and, in an abrupt stumble and spill over the window ledge, swings and struggles briefly against the aluminum siding.

The sun casts long, undefined shadows across the faintly frosted grass, and the birds quiet as they begin the business of winter feeding. A dog rises in its kennel at the prompting of a stray breeze, and picks its way over droppings and ammonia-stained concrete to snuff through the chain-link. Several yards away, Scofield's gloves lie drying rapidly in the morning air.

∾

In his office, Father Robert sat down to open his mail. Before reading them, he opened all of the letters with his pinky finger—letter openers always seemed to disappear. He recognized Cam's writing immediately. Her downstrokes were long and severely slanted, often obscuring the writing on the next line. Her loops were not loops at all, but almost impossibly perfect parallelograms—signs of aggression, creativity, and deep emotional disturbance. In the last year, he had gotten several letters from her. First a card with smiling music notes on it arrived to thank him and Sister Gwen for taking care of her. Then he received a couple of letters on purple stationery thanking him for his help in getting her into Saint Teresa's High School in Chicago and telling him how much she liked her counselor, how nice her father's girlfriend was, and how impressed she was with the nun who directed the school band. One letter spoke of her uncle's suicide, telling Father Robert nothing he hadn't seen in the papers or heard from word of mouth—the man had been found by an old K-9 trainer, hanging out a third-floor window by a dog leash. Apparently he killed himself in fear of being arrested for molesting his cousin's daughter, who had been staying with him and run away. Dog food was piled high in each kennel, and each dog had been given several bowls of water. Police found the sinks and bathtub overflowing, all the windows left open to the blizzards of spring, and sheets of water frozen across the floors. The state police purchased the dogs and property as a future county K-9 unit.

This new letter was postmarked Colorado, written on the stationery of a Christian summer camp for girls. Camille wrote that there was little opportunity to play her flute, but she supposed a summer without music might be good for her. The girls did sing plenty, before and after meals, during Mass, and of course at campfire. She and several others had the opportunity to study their catechism, and in a few weeks she would be celebrating her first Eucharist. She knew he would agree that this would make her grandmother happy.

She had said something similar at the bus station, stepping off the bus pleasantly and saying, "I suppose Grandma's glad I came to you." She held out a wallet and flute case. "All I have," she said, grinning. "You'd better take this," and she handed him the wallet. He and Sister Gwen phoned parents of high school girls to borrow some clothes for Cam until arrangements could be made with her father. They put her on a plane the next day.

Lunch in the rectory kitchen had been taxing for all of them. He and Sister watched as Cam sat by the sunny window, her body buzzing with agitation, her skin shaded blue and gray in the bright light, features blurred and shiny with old makeup, eyelids red with irritation. She tried jokes with them—"You two married?" and "I didn't think priests went to the bathroom," after which she'd apologize, "Just kidding," or "I must be real tired." While it was obvious to him that she was traumatized, Father Robert was not good at getting people to talk. Usually people came to him already prepared to unburden, or to gossip. They came to the Center because they needed advice, counsel, or legal support. While they sometimes needed a little prompting before they opened up, they had come because they wanted something, and they eventually talked, or left. Cam had already gotten what she wanted—a bus trip, a place to stay, and a phone call to her father. She prattled about walking the ten miles to her old house just to have a look at it while she was in town. She wanted to see the cemetery too, but the house was most important. She appeared at once so fatigued and yet maddeningly alert that he wondered if she was on amphetamines. "Why don't you rest?" was all he could say, but Sister Gwen, outgoing and cunning, said, "Nonsense. She's bushy-tailed. She was just about to tell us what brought her here." Sister Gwen had no time for those who delayed the unpleasant. She had the electrical kindness of a head nurse, administering comments like painful and efficient medicine.

Cam pushed away her half-eaten meal and asked for a cigarette. And then, in a look of genuine shame mingled with adolescent theatrics, she crumpled to the floor in tears. "I can't, I can't," she said, "I'll never be able." Sister Gwen led her into the sitting room and shut the door, leaving Father Robert the dishes. While Father cleaned the kitchen, he recalled his earlier misgivings about the girl and found his confidence in his intuition greatly bolstered. When he turned off the water in the sink, he could hear the steady and clear sound of Cam's voice, softly plodding through a narrative. His faith in Christ's effect on her through him was confirmed when, after he prayed for her during the entire drive to the airport, she thanked him, Father Robert, almost exclusively. When she wrote, she wrote to him and no one else. Sister Gwen, of course, deserved most if not all the praise for the two days, but his prayers and dedication to child victims were part of the whole of his life, his attempt at approaching the eternity of Christ's love. Whatever Cam reacted to, either his constancy or Sister's frankness and nurturing, she was seeing the love of God.

All during their correspondence, he saw her awareness of Christ grow. In one letter she wrote him that she had been studying the female saints and found herself drawn to those whose lives were examples of penitential practices, who spurned the flesh and strove to be ravished by God's purity. She was searching for a confirmation name and couldn't decide between Rose of Lima, who invented numerous and creative methods of self-torture in order to conform to her God, Sister Margaret Mary, who with a knife and candle carved in her breast the name of the Lord, or Maria Goretti, whose story of choosing death over rape brought Cam to tears. She composed a song in Goretti's honor, but wasn't ready to share it with anyone. Her enthusiasm made Father uneasy. He folded the letter and returned it to its envelope. He took out a pencil, sharpened it over an ashtray he kept in his top drawer to catch the shavings, and began a reply. "No love should victimize," he wrote. "Martyrdom is rarely practical." He thought of drawing up a list of sane female saints to send to her, but never did.

Father Robert read in the letter from the Christian summer camp that the girls had gone on a two-mile hike that had the stations of the cross spaced along the trail, and then Cam wrote: "Last week I realized that God has always been with me, as if in the air, but I never knew who or what it was—too many dark forms in the way. I sometimes felt that His presence was about to kill me, but I see now that those were moments of comfort, God's way of promising He would never let my unhappiness swallow me. I believe that we are God's fantasies, and that ghosts are His remembrances, which means that when I die, I won't join with my mother after all, but it won't matter. I'll go into the memory banks, and one day maybe He'll remember me or her or both of us together—walking up the stairs in our matching blue nightgowns side by side—but in the meantime I have to live like Mary, who was probably just a girl like me, really, offering herself and her body, visited when she was vulnerable in her sleep by God in His sleep, as though they were mutual dreams. So I figure, there is no such thing as love, just an awareness of oneness."

It occurred then to Father Robert that Mary was the first tabernacle of Christ's body. He saw her capsized, her body paralyzed with sleep, and heard her say, "Let it be done to me," she somehow sensing that the specter was more than benign. How much of her certitude was will, faith, foolishness, coercion, or madness, Father Robert didn't know, but her cooperation in spite of the outrageousness was among the marvels of that moment. He saw her sleeping form rise and kneel on her bed in outward grace, bend her head to the buffets of an apparition, stutter words of submission, and lie down under the cumbersome press of the One who dreamed her.

about the author

At twenty-six, Elisabeth Rose wrote *Body Sharers* while completing her Master of Fine Arts degree at Penn State University. She now teaches fiction writing at Penn State and has received several awards, including the 1991 Washington Prize for Fiction. Her fiction credits include stories in *Feminist Studies* and *Valley Women's Voice*, and her criticism has appeared in *Studies in American Jewish Literature*. She lives in State College, Pennsylvania, with the author Joe Schall, their daughter Delaney, a Border Collie, and three cats.